ABWW13

The Alamo Bay Writers' Workshop Anthology

2013

ABWW13

The Alamo Bay Writers' Workshop Anthology

2013

Lowell Mick White, Editor

ALAMO BAY PRESS

SEADRIFT·AUSTIN

Some of the work appearing in this anthology has been previously published:
"To a Red Leaf" appeared in *Maple Leaf Rag IV*
"Detroit: America's Ciudad Juarez" appeared on *The Huffington Post*
"Deep Eddy" appeared in *R-KV-R-Y*
"Delbert's Tattoo" appeared in *Holy Roller*

Cover Art: "Barbara Jordan's Guardian Angel," by Reji Thomas
Back Cover Photos: Pamela Booton
Book Design: Buffalo Times Productions

For orders and information:
Alamo Bay Press
Pamela Booton, Director
825 W 11th Ste 114
Austin, Texas 78701
www.alamobaywritersworkshop.com

Library of Congress Control Number: 2014900481
ISBN-13: 9780615950570

Dedications

For Pamela Booton, for making things happen.
 —Lowell Mick White

To my niece Jessica Reich, author of "The Hidden Poet," and to all those hidden poets out there.
 —Pamela Booton

Close Gitmo! Clean up Bhopal!
 —Diane Wilson

Contents

ABWW13

The Alamo Bay Writers' Workshop Anthology

2013

Lowell Mick White

Introduction

The Alamo Bay Writers' Workshop began in June 2012, at Bubba's Cajun Seafood in Seadrift, Texas. Over dinner I was sitting across from environmental and social activist/writer Diane Wilson and I said something like, "We should teach a workshop together sometime." Diane agreed.

Normally, an idea like that would have stopped right there—two writers at dinner expressing vague ideas about future collaborations. Normally, writers would continue to eat shrimp and drink beer and tell tales. But it wasn't a normal evening. Also sitting at that table was Pamela Booton, a financial advisor and patron of the arts, and she overheard our vague ideas. Pamela is a doer and a maker, and she was taken by the idea. We ended up spending the rest of the evening and the next day brainstorming ways to make the workshop a reality.

And a little over a year later—in July 2013—the workshop happened. Pamela was the Director, and Diane and I, joined by novelist Larry Heinemann and poet Lee Meitzen Grue, were instructors. Accomplished writer and academic dean Dr. Hazel Ward moderated. Renowned artist Reji Thomas lectured on the creative process. From the initial brainstorming our goal was to move beyond the traditional sit-in-a-circle-and-be-nice workshop, to offer participants more than mildly encouraging peer critiques. We wanted to offer writing instruction with a focus on social justice and the development of writers' voices in the global community. We all believe in this, and we all work toward social justice in our own lives and writing—Diane, with her commitment to the environment and people of the Gulf Coast and her fight against injustice throughout the world; Lee, a native of New Orleans who founded the Quorum Club and fought for civil rights and who has used her voice as a Katrina spokesperson; Larry, a longtime advocate for the veterans of America's wars; and myself, a writer, teacher, and advocate for creative writing in prison. And thanks to Pamela's work, we moved beyond writing itself to include music and visual art, always looking for ways to connect art and social justice.

The workshop was, I think, a terrific success.

From our venue at Rio Far Niente atop a river bluff east of Austin, looking back west upstream at the hills of the city, we filled two and a half days with literature and art and music and thought and camaraderie.

This volume is a record of those days. Here you will read pieces that are personal favorites, or work that has been completed and revised in the aftermath of the workshop, or work that was inspired by the workshop, and, in some cases, just the raw notebooks offering what the writer felt and saw at the workshop. All of the writing in this anthology comes from the heart.

Rebecca Byrd Arthur

The Guardian

You may only see me
from the corner of your eye
Backstage, barely lit; a shadow
Know that I
am
the Guardian.

Glance toward me I'll disappear
Most never even know I'm here
I'm packing heat and supernatural powers
With you especially during the difficult hours
I am
the Guardian.

Awake, asleep, out 'til dawn
An easy day or an unproductive one
I am your intercedent to the angry, vile and mean
The fiercest angel you have ever seen.
Yes, I am
the Guardian.

Locked and loaded I quietly await
My daily duty, my joyful fate.
Watching over mortal frailties
Seeing the oddfellows squirm.
The majority of human-kind has yet to learn
I am
the Guardian.

I dwell in good but it's just for sport
'Cause I'm used to dealing with life's other sort
As a soul of the streets, I prefer to hide
Appealing to the light from the darker side.
I remain
the Guardian.

The Lens

The Lens.
That prism that filters the light
      into your life
Can be so affected by events
      not of your own making.

Galileo and his stars,
      Your mother's upbringing,
            or even Haiti's tectonic plates
               could not be stopped.

What matters is the light,
and how you let it in.

This soaking up—
emits its own light
      onto others
Converting and returning energy
into compassion, love, hope, hate,
      anger, depression, greed,
      anxiety, and envy.

It has many forms,
but the way you see it
All depends on
      The Lens.

Vessels

Trés Amigas—three vessels, we.
Bound together by hope and hill country geography,
Seeking ballast for balance of circumstance
Each rigged for gales, scoffing at winds of chance.

That is what friends are supposed to do
Ferry through the fog,
See each wave through
Always there to help mend the sails.

Thirteen years passed in the blink of an eye
Canvases showed wear, swabbed boards ran dry.
Barely sea-worthy, feeling aged and old
Warped main and Mizzen masts, holds filled with gold.

It has taken til now for
these old friends to say
They've enjoyed this metaphor,
but there's been a mistake...

We are vessels, yes; clay molded fine—
Just one homonym away from the sea-faring kind.
Fragile, just the same.

We vessels within where souls dwell,
Cargos of living fire inside a fragile shell.
Culmination of water and earthen clay
Born to live and to ebb away.

Linda Caplin

Selections from a Writer's Notebook

The King of Mombasa

The heir to the throne of Mombasa was listening to music as he jumped up-down on the mattress. He wanted the others to join him but they couldn't understand his jargon and they were stragglers anyway. Teenagers with their malignant thoughts not being willing to do the two year old's bidding. Phooey on the Big Kids! I'm going to be King of Mombasa: then bring over the Big Kids and then they'll have to jump on the mattress w/me—or else!

22

22, Never a significant number to me, like 13 or 18 or 21, all milestones. Nor was it my birthday, 6/15. Not my mother's age, nor my father's, but that day it became a significant number for me. Russ and I had been invited to join the Peace Corps, still very new. In fact, we were in a group of volunteers called Ecuador 3, the 1st replacement group of volunteers for Ecuador. Your stint was for 2 years and we had flown to the new York City to win w/the other volunteers in our group before we headed to Puerto Rico for a month's training. We were going to be in an outward bound camp called Camp Crozier after the 1st volunteer who had died. Cheery thought! We wondered if there would be any other married couples. There were 5 more, but 2 got deselected before going to Ecuador. Peace Corps jargon for you're out. We spent the morning meeting other volunteers & instructors, then broke for lunch. I suggested to Russ that we go downstairs to the little pub in the hotel, get a beer & a sandwich. I said I'll bet they have the TV on to watch the parade. They did. We sat at the bar on Nov. 22, 1963 and watched as our young president was assassinated. Hearing Walter Cronkite say, The President is dead was so stunning. That 11/22 we walked the streets of NYC w/other PCVs, seeing Broadway dark. Nov. 22nd, we remember.

Untitled

Looking out the window at the peaceful scene of grass, trees, hills, a white bird, I noticed a solitary figure walking this way in the field below.

I could tell he was a man by the way he carried himself; the strides he made—not like a woman. He had a slight limp but he still walked well, no cane, standing proud. I couldn't tell what he was wearing at first, but it looked familiar. He disappeared into the trees, so I went outside to see if I could spot him. He came out of the trees and started slowly up the hill. He was wearing a uniform, an army uniform. But this uniform was not the camouflage type of today's soldiers, nor did he look like a soldier from the Viet Nam era. Instead, as he came slowly up the hill, I could see he was wearing an Eisenhower jacket, an officer's cap and jump boots. On his sleeve was the Double A patch of the 82nd Airborne! He was a paratrooper from W.W. II. My heart started pounding. I had met many old troopers from the 82nd of W.W. II, but this man was young, in his 20's. Where did he get the uniform? As he came up over the hill I saw the medals, the Purple Heart, the cluster indicating he was a major, the patch of the Devil in Baggy Pants. That was from a German officer's diary about the battle of Anzio. Then I looked at his rugged, handsome face. It was that of a man who died in Italy at Chiunzi Pass on 9/24/43. I called out to him—Daddy Bob!

Lee Edwards

August (Lyrics)

Fly on the windowsill—too hot to fly
Old men at the Texaco—too hot to lie
My old AC up and died where it stood
Oh, August ain't lookin' too good

The day that you left, you said, "It's for the best"
But I don't feel blessed, just alone and depressed
Since the first of July, it only rains when I cry
Oh, August ain't lookin' too good

There's a hole in my heart; there's a hole in my mind
There's a peace I can't find, though Lord knows I've tried
In the deep end of summer, oh, I'm goin' under
With an unholy hole in my heart
No, August ain't lookin' too good

Cool of the pool, shade of the porch
Others find refuge; I'm still scorched
If sweat cleans the soul, maybe I can be whole
Honey, tell me—am I clean enough?

There's a hole in my heart; there's a hole in my mind
There's a peace I can't find, though Lord knows I've tried
In the deep end of summer, oh, I'm goin' under
With an unholy hole in my heart
No, August ain't lookin' too good

The trouble with Texas is summer comes due
Trouble with love is losin' you
This August ain't lookin' too good to me

Faded Town (Lyrics)

There's a one room church, the heart of town
Paint is peeling, but it's sacred ground
The faithful come to sing and cry—
"Oh, by and by, Lord, by and by"
"Rock of Ages," "Abide with Me,"
"Just As I Am," "He Walks with Me"
And now the sun goes down on this faded town

Faded bar, the edge of town
The faithful come to drink and drown
Jukebox pours a round of country songs
Forgotten feelings come back just as strong
"Faded Love" plays just once more
Couples sway on wooden boards
Now the sun goes down on this faded town

The young folks go, the old folks stay
This sweet old town just fades away

Porch swing sways in dying light
Weathered hands meet and hold on tight
Faded rose in his tattoo
Where her name's written in Navy blue
Silver locket, worn and scarred
Holds his picture against her heart
And now the sun goes down on this faded town
Now the sun goes down on this faded town

False Promise

He made his first false promise in front of God and everybody.

It felt good.

It gave him that rush
    that comes with believing he was
    the kind of person who would follow through.

And the woman,
    who drank up the promise like a cool spring
    discovered in the midst of love's parched desert,
    felt the rush of believing—
    believing she could turn a sow's ear into a silk purse.

It felt good.

Elsewhere, God and everybody felt a bit uncomfortable.
'Cuz there'd be hell to pay.

    Eventually.

But for that moment,
    for that moment,
    the two of them abandoned themselves to the dance,
    twirling on the brink.

It felt good.

God Made Of

My friend, Tom, has a god made of music
Flowing
Beautiful
A river—mysterious, strong

My ex, Carry, has a god made of rules
Who shows her the lines to color between
Helps her keep the chaos at bay
Helps keep the critics away

My healer, Kenneth, has a god made of sex
And ecstasy
And grieving
And connection
Fire and earth

Coach Roy has a god made of football
Discipline, teamwork, competition
Turns out God loves winners and hates losers
So be a winner

My neighbor, Marcus, has a god made of gold
He clings to it at night for warmth

And Dad has a god made of duty
And duty calls and calls and calls

And me, I got a god made of questions
And hurt
And longing
Vague around the edges and vague around the middle

But my dear friend, Linda, has a god made of love
Linda has a god made of love
Linda has a god made of love

The Silence (Lyrics)

The silence hurts my ears
The silence hurts your heart
The silence screams through this two-story house
    and tears the place apart

The anger fills your eyes
The anger kills my hope
The anger shreds the thinning threads at the end of my rope

Do we just give up?
Do we just give in?
Whoa, oh, oh, oh, oh
Will we let the silence win?

Remember how we talked?
We had so much to say
I remember every loving word,
but is that enough to stay?

Do we just give up?
Do we just give in?
Whoa, oh, oh, oh, oh
Will we let the silence win?

Are these the last words we'll speak?
Oh, talk to me…tell me

Do we just give up?
Do we just give in?
Whoa, oh, oh, oh, oh
Will we let the silence win?
Whoa, oh, oh, oh, oh
Have we let the silence win?

Grace Fleming

from In Love with Salt Cedar

Buela Rose saw the square hole at the bottom of the wall on a bright winter day and knew that lives would collide in the coming storm. This was the third day of waking with an uneasiness in the earliest hours before dawn. She sighed heavily knowing sleep would not return until after sunset that evening. Her widow's bed creaked as she rolled over and pushed herself up. She sat with legs hanging, feet searching for the chanclas that her grandson, called Birkenstocks. He gave her the shoes last Christmas. She loved their soft blue straps across the tops of her feet and the way the soles wrapped her heels. In their New Mexico winter she wore them with her heavy wool socks. On this cool morning in May, she had them buckled over cotton.

It was four thirty in the morning. She always woke at four thirty. Without turning on the lights, the rotund old woman with thick grey hair to her waist stood slowly and made her way through the old house with its spacious rooms and wood floors that knew the footsteps of five generations of the Baca family. She turned on the kitchen light and filled the teapot with water when she heard the dull scratching on Zachary's door down the hall telling her their dog, Mysti, was ready to start her day.

Buela went to open the door for the fat, black dog. A few minutes later, the two plump figures ambled out to the screened porch at the front of the house with a tray of hot tea and biscuits. As they settled in, Rose pulled her shawl closer and tossed the ends over her shoulders. Mysti gave one muffled thump of her tail against the layers of dhurrie rugs that made her bed.

Buela Rose poured a cup of tea and gave the dog a biscuit. A moment later a wave of physical sensations mixed with many emotions passed across her heart. "Something is coming, Mysti. I can't see it yet, but, I can feel it." The dog gave one loud thump of its tail. Buela answered, "Yeah. I know. It's a big one this time. We better go say our prayers."

Soon they made their way through the dark house without lights and stepped into the backyard where a wide swath of stepping stones and desert clover soaked up the moonlight across the back of the house. The stands of salt cedar on the other side of three rental cabins about fifty yards away moved back and forth in the night breezes. The old woman and dog stepped lightly on the flat stones that led to the twelve foot high wall of vines at the far end of the house. The full moon drew sharp shadows of a woman and a dog walking to the garden.

Buela Rose reached for the latch on the only part of the fence that was spared from the grape vines. The liquid moonlight polished the metal chain link gate. The gate moaned as she pulled the latch upward, and stepped into the garden. In the darkness, she chanted and danced and prayed without connection to time.

Late that morning, Buela was chopping pork when Zachary made his way into the kitchen. She knew he always woke up hungry. She said, "have some cereal. That'll hold you. It won't take too long for the posole to cook."

"K." Zachary poured cereal and seated himself at the kitchen table. He said, "Buela Rose, I need to talk. I been thinking."

The old woman twisted at the waist to look at the young man. He rolled his gentle brown eyes up at her while chewing. His long black hair was pulled into a bun on top of his head. He leaned his tall figure over the table looking relaxed and much older than his seventeen years. Most people assumed that losing his father when he was only thirteen had forced the boy to grow up fast, but his grandmother knew that he was an old soul. He had never really been young. Still, she worried when he started a conversation that way. She asked, "What is it?"

He chewed a huge spoonful of flakes and nuts and raisins and swallowed. "I think I should wait a year to start college. I want to just work full time and then go."

A dozen thoughts raced through Buela's mind and they all started with either "No" or "You can't." She thought about his father and calmed herself down. She continued chopping pork. Finally she said, "Don't get sidetracked. College is your full time job. It starts in August."

"I could save a lot of money in a year. Then I could use it for school next year."

"When did you start worrying about money? We have money for your college." She put down the knife and turned to face the boy. The greasy hand that had held the pork while she cut now dangled with fingers curled upward like a dead tarantula. She asked, "Are you worried about the motel?"

Their eyes met for a long gaze. These were the two most stubborn members of the family. They both knew what that meant.

He said, "Yeah. Sorta."

She asked, "and about your Buela, too?"

"Yeah. Mostly."

"Well, don't. The family has been talking about it. We'll figure something out."

The boy had quit eating, his bowl still half full. "I'm staying here this year."

"You need college in this world today. You gotta get college." She turned back to the cutting board, her heart filled with worry.

"I will get college, just not right away."

A few hours later, when her grandson said his goodbye to go to work at the family diner in town, Buela Rose pulled her mobile phone from her skirt pocket. She decided to call her youngest son first. Freddie knew how to reach Zachary when the rest of the family couldn't. And so began several hours of the Baca family two-stepping through cyberspace together to figure out how to get Zachary to go to college in Albuquerque in fall. Calls were not enough and so they texted and turned to Facebook and Twitter. Some even resorted to email. There were at least a dozen of them lighting up their corner of the universe and beyond. Freddie even managed a Skyped conversation with Zachary's mom who was stationed in Belgium with the Army. Late in the afternoon the cousins began to weigh in with views that differed greatly from the elders. By evening there were at least two dozen people involved in the matter.

Buela knew Zachary had turned off his phone early in the day, so she was surprised to see a calling coming in from him around eight o'clock that evening.

She answered the phone. "Hello."

Zachary said, "Buela Rose, there's a customer here looking for a place to stay. I think the motel rooms are all full or reserved. Do you want to rent her a cabin?"

Buela said, "I can do that."

Buela Rose put fresh linens and toiletries in one of the cabins while she waited for Zachary and the guest. She checked the paper towels, coffee filters, and the like. She took her time. The drive from town was thirty minutes. She was back in the house when she heard tires crunching along the gravel drive. She watched them from the front door as they got out of the car.

The woman was petite. As they climbed the steps to the porch, the woman's yellow skinny jeans and dark blue tee shirt showed a youthful figure. She had a cloth bag hanging from one shoulder to her thigh, keys in one hand and a cell phone nested in the other. She had large black eyes like the Moors that once occupied the Spaniards. Her eyelashes were long and thick without the help of mascara.

Zachary said, "Buela Rose, this is Lydia. She wants a nice place to stay tonight."

Buela Rose responded, "Come on in. I made up Carmela's cabin while I was waiting for you to get here."

Zachary smiled, his eyes squinting almost closed. "Carmela leaves good karma."

Lydia asked, "Who's Carmela?"

Buela Rose asked for a credit card and quickly made her way out of the living room to her office in a far corner of the house. She didn't want personal conversation with customers. She returned with paperwork and a pen to find Lydia standing in the middle of the living room alone. When Rose handed the pen to Lydia, there was an instant when both women held the pen together. In that moment Rose saw a dozen strong images of Lydia at different ages. She saw Lydia as a girl playing in a river with her parents; crying alone in bed; beaming in a traditional wedding dress; falling on a rocky hillside; playing with small children and an old man; a visit from a dark angel; serious illness. The images were powerful but one of them stole the old woman's breath. Rose took a moment to find balance as Lydia signed the paperwork. The old woman tucked the images in her heart for safe-keeping.

Lydia clicked the pen and handed it back to Rose, but the old woman didn't want to touch it again. "You can just leave it there on the piano."

Lydia placed the pen on top of the piano and winced as she pulled back her hand to rub the opposite arm. "I'm pretty stiff from sitting in a car all day."

Buela Rose said, "Or from a scar that you don't have yet."

Lydia flinched with pain as a look of confusion crossed her pale face.

The two women headed toward the kitchen so they could exit the back door. Zachary rushed in to hand off a bright green tee shirt to Lydia. He noted his grandmother's raised eyebrow.

Rose asked Lydia, "Don't you have luggage?"

Lydia said, "I didn't know when I left home this morning that I would be traveling today."

The old woman looked closely at the younger one. She saw shadows but couldn't see what they hid. They felt like the shadows of chaos. They didn't seem to bear any ill will. Still, Rose wondered if someone was looking for Lydia. Was this new guest in trouble?

Rose said, "Follow close. The moon's not up yet. It's too dark to see your feet. It'll take a second before we can see the lights from the cabin."

A couple of minutes later, as she unlocked the cabin and let the young woman in, Rose turned back to see the dog silhouetted in the kitchen door. She knew the dog would stand just like that until Rose was safely back at the house. Then its tail would knock hard against the kitchen door.

Back at her house, Rose found Zachary laid out in a recliner watching tv. His long body extended the length of the chair and still his heels hung off the end of the foot rest. She reclined in the other chair and they watched tv together until the next commercial.

She asked, "What do you know about the new guest?"

Zachary said, "She lives in Austin. She was on a freeway this morning and just kept driving. She's never been to New Mexico."

Rose said, "Impulsive."

"Yeah."

"You don't usually give your clothes to guests."

"I don't usually meet someone who just started driving and five hundred miles later wondered what was in New Mexico."

Rose said, "Be careful, Grandson."

"I know, Buela. I see the shadows, too."

She reached out and patted his shoulder. She said, "I'm going to bed. I just wanted to make sure your antennae's working. With your crazy talk about not going to college in fall, I'm afraid you're knocked off your rocker."

Zachary looked up. For a moment his eyes squinted closed with a grin. She could see he was enjoying their battle.

He said, "Antennae's working, Buela Rose. Good night."

She knew he watched her as she headed for her bedroom. It was hard to tell who worried more, the young man about his grandmother or the old woman about her grandson.

Alone in her bedroom, Rose turned her thoughts back to the woman in the cabin. The images from Lydia's life had been clear, yet, one included Rose's life. And that was the most curious of them all. She wondered what this woman brought to their world. She also wondered what they had to offer besides a nice little cabin on the edge of a stand of salt cedar.

In the dark hours of the next morning, Buela Rose woke without the feeling of unease that had nipped at her for days. Her work was now laid out before her.

Ken Fontenot

On a Flight to Lafeyette

Squeezed in the plane, our sleeves touch.
The chilliness of early March,
our father being laid to rest tomorrow.
We'll stay with his sister,
not in such good health herself.
Coffee will be served, Cajun style.
Aunt Sister will walk the tray to each.

I'll give the funeral oration you helped
me write. St. Augustine Church
is expected to be full,
for he knew almost everyone.
My attire: a borrowed suit.
Your dress was worn by our mother
at the funeral of her own mother.

Sheila, take my hand.
No one else here knows our story.

To a Red Leaf

The months turn into eternities,
but looking back it all happened so fast.
My first success riding a bicycle.
My first time driving a car.
My first love, lost irretrievably.
Learning how to write a poem.
A biology final for which I got an A.
The death of my parents.
And now I'm my own parent.
More stars make the biggest difference.
I'm where soul and spirit intersect.
I'm wherever Ceres has saddened.

Cracks are for the light to push through.
Leaves are there to surrender to autumn.
A red leaf is a thing of beauty.
Even though, or especially because, it's vanishing.

Lori Spence Galloway

Sleep

Sleep

While I wait
for sleep
to quiet my restless mind
I marvel
at the lush petals of darkness
at the clarity of sounds lost
in the cacophony of day
in the richness of nothing
and everything.
And as sleep
slowly settles my thoughts
I hear the music
of silence
I feel the softness
of the petals
soothe my soul.

Evening at the Shore

Reclining on a mattress of sand
like the heir to the throne of Mombasa,
I watch the stragglers come in from the surf
the air malignant with the heat of the day.

Floating in the wind
music from a foreign land
the words like jargon from an unknown trade.

My army
the crabs
scurry to a feast of scraps
while shorebirds thin their ranks.

Red- and green-eyed giants troll the bay for fish
as the sun slowly settles in for a swim
tossing its blanket of pink and orange skyward.

I rise to leave
as the blanket fades to ink
and the moon scatters the stars like sea glass
across the sky.

Performance

The curtain opens with thunderous applause from the skies
Vacationing clouds have left their summer homes
to spill the remnants of their time at sea
Members of the audience spread their branches
acknowledging every drop
as squirrels perform a ballet in pure joy
Song birds in the orchestra fill the air with native music
while a steady drum keeps rhythm in the background
And as night draws the curtain closed
the clouds move on to their next venue
and the saturated earth breathes a sigh of relief.

Lee Meitzen Grue

Chapter One, Blood at the Root

Elliot heard them say it. He heard them say it lots of times.

He said, "Moo, who is High John the Conqueror?" She closed her face down like a rat trap with the rat in it.

She said, "Where you hear that, Elliot?"

He said, "I hear it lots of times."

"Little pitchers got big ears," she said as she swished soap around in a mason jar, rinsed and laid it upside down on the dish drain before answering. "You better let that subject lay."

"Took told Hall the iceman that Camilla Jane's got High John the Conqueror all locked up and that she can have any man she wants because she's got him, and I don't know him. He's not from High Castle. Is he from New Orleans?"

"Yes, sir. You got it right. That's where he's from."

She was laughing a mean little laugh she laughed sometimes when she knew something—like what he was going to get for his birthday and it was something he didn't want.

"Moo," he said, "I'm worried about your soul. You're old and you're mean. It won't be long before you're dead and some people won't be sorry to see you go. I hope you have somebody other than this family to say masses for the repose of your soul."

She turned her back on him, and her back could close down even better than her face. "I'm going next door," he said to her back. She didn't answer but he had to tell her anyway or he'd get in trouble.

Elliot climbed over the back fence because it was the shortcut and the handiest way to go. Aunt Mag's kitchen was out back. He climbed through her butterbean vine strung up by a string lattice on the back gallery, his thin body passing through without knocking off a bean.

He ate a couple of raw butter beans, not only because they were half decent to eat but because he liked to watch Took at the end of the season store the dried beans in a mason jar with tobacco to keep the weevils out of next year's seed. He felt obliged. In order to keep seed somebody had to eat butterbeans.

From the gallery he can see Took in the kitchen walking slow to the coal oil stove, to the sink, to the ice box—going back and forth because she never remembers what she wants to get the first time. She's making coffee and something else. He lays low so he can see what she's doing.

She walks to the ice box and takes out a couple of eggs, then she walks over to the kitchen cabinet and takes down a batter bowl. Then she walks back to the ice box and gets the milk. She must make ten trips around the kitchen before she's got everything she needs. The last thing she gets is the vanilla bean so Elliot knows she's going to make French toast.

"You going to make French toast?" he asks through the screen.

"Where you come from, Creeping Jesus? Come on in here. Can't you make some noise when you walk?"

He comes in to watch. She sticks the vanilla bean in a bowl of milk, which swallows it up, but he can see a tan stain in the milk where it's beginning to work. She turns around slow and starts back toward her old rocker with its rusty-looking blue seat cover. There's something about her seat that looks like the seat of the rocker, soft and sort of worn. She grabs the arms of the rocker, lets go with her feet and falls down into it. She sighs in time to the creak of the rocker. "Now, what do you want?"

"Who's High John the Conqueror?"

"You don't talk about High John unless you got a use for him and then, you don't talk about him loud." She leans forward and looks into his face. Took smells like coal oil and bacon grease. The smell of it comes out of the pores of her skin and grabs him before she puts out both arms and says, "Come on, Sugar, sit on my lap and I'll tell you." Elliot gets on her lap, but his feet are hanging over onto the floor. He knows he's too big but he likes the bacon grease and coal oil smell. He leans back and she tells him in his ear.

"High John the Conqueror is a man root. He a man when he wants to be and he a root when he wants to be."

"Where's Camilla Jane got him locked up?"

"Who said she got him locked up?" She looks down her nose at him, pulling together the dark skin around her eyes, which are little and dull as four o'clock seeds.

"You said that to Hall."

She grabbed both his arms and held onto him. "You don't go saying that. Miss Mag says they's no Hoodoo here and they's no Hoodoo here. So you watch what you say, Sir, or something bad's liable to happen to you."

"I won't say anything. My lips are sealed with an X." And he showed her with his finger making a big X over his mouth.

"Get up, Mister. You too heavy for old Took. Too heavy." She let him go and moved to finish the French toast. She beat two eggs into the vanilla milk then soaked pieces of French bread in the milk and egg mixture. She fished the bread out with a slotted spoon, put it into a hot iron skillet, fried one side in butter, flipped it once with a spatula, fried the other side and moved it onto a piece of brown paper bag on the enamel shelf of the stove. In a few minutes, she had five pieces of French toast laid out on the paper. She let him shake granulated sugar over it with a teaspoon. He held the handle of the spoon in the upturned palm of his left hand. To suit her, he had to slap his left wrist with little taps of his right hand to get just the right amount of sugar on the French toast. After it looked right, she moved the toast onto a small white plate with yellow and orange narcissus flowers painted on it. She poured a big cup of coffee and put in four tablespoons of condensed milk then gave him the tray to take upstairs to Camilla Jane.

"She sick," Took said.

He got out of the kitchen screen by pushing it with his bare foot. Took helped him but he had to walk down the back gallery and all the way up the side gallery by himself, open the screen door to the hall, close it, and then open the wooden door to the attic stairs. The stairs were steep, narrow, and hot. He had to do all this without spilling a drop because sure as he did Camilla Jane would jump out of bed and let the toads out of her mouth.

Whenever Elliot did anything for Camilla Jane he could hear Moo's voice in his head, "Old Miss Elise had four daughters: Your mother's the best, but she's wore out from miscarriages. Two of them live up North and Mag a throwback. Now we got this disgusting generation—you and your cousin Camilla Jane. She some sort of remnant, messed up piece at the end of a bolt of good material. Her and her Hoodoo sister. I don't know why you want to hang over there all the time."

But he knew why he hung around. Why he wanted to go up the dark stairs that smelled of old secret things to Camilla Jane's room on the right at the head of the stairs.

The other side, at the top of the landing, was a junk room. He always stopped by this wall, where there was a hole like a rat had been chewing into the brown, papery composition board. Every time he came up he peeled off another piece. He could see in deep, count the ends of the layers, see how the walls were made, how each piece of paper held up the other pieces into something that appeared solid. Except for the hole he'd made, you'd never know it was all paper. The door to the junk room had a brown china door knob. He wanted to go in there, look at the yellowed sheet music, read Sea Serpents, in the box of old books, but he had to bring the coffee to Camilla Jane because he was going to ask her.

She was sleeping on her stomach, wearing white batiste pajama with ruffles on the legs, one knee bent up to her chin. When he came in he shoved the door with his foot and struck the end of her metal bed with his heel. It rang like a gong. She turned over and kicked off the sheet. He could see a big reddish-brown stain at the top of her wrinkled pajama leg. At the other end of the bed he could see her black hair, sweaty curls stuck to her face. Her skin looked thick. It had a special kind of pink to it that could look good with her hair was all fluffed out and she had on lipstick. Right now she looked hot and cross as two sticks.

"Well, if it isn't Skinny-Marinky-Dink making enough noise to wake the dead. Aren't you sweet, bringing me breakfast in bed—French toast and cold coffee. Same thing every day. Took only knows how to make two things—both cold. She' the only cook in the world knows how to cook without heat."

She sat up and motioned him over. "Jesus, Elliot, every time I look at you you're skinnier. I hope you fill out by the ninth grade or some dog's liable to carry you off for a bone." She grabbed the French toast and started tearing it into little pieces and stuffing it into her mouth with her fingers. He didn't say anything. Just looked around. Camilla Jane always ate like she was starving. There was a big picture of her twin, Pamella Jeanne, on the dresser, a piece of palm from Palm Sunday stuck in the metal frame; a plate of dried red beans sat in front of the picture. Keeled over on its back, a big outside roach lay on top of the beans. Elliot didn't know if the beans had killed the roach but they looked poisonous enough to kill a cow. There was a circle of flour around the plate and the picture, two burned down candles in front of it. In the frame Pamella Jeanne looked timid, milky-faced, not much like Camilla Jane. She was only four years old when she died from stringing oleander blossoms and biting off the stems. Moo said, "Colored kids always die from swallowing lye and white kids die from stringing flowers."

"Why don't you go now, Sugar. I have things to do." Camilla Jane gave him her sweet smile.

"Where's High John?" he asked.

She put down the bread and stared at him. She didn't growl but she might have. She looked like a dog does when it's eating and thinks you want to take its food.

"What did you say?"

"High John the Conqueror Root—where do you keep him?"

"Get yourself out of here. You ask stupid questions about something you don't know anything about. I'm going to tell your mother how smart and sassy you act and Moo's going to whip your butt."

"You tell my mother I'm sassy and I'm going to tell Aunt Mag you mess around with Hoodoo and you've got a Hoodoo altar to Pamella Jeanne in your room."

"Now wait a minute, Elliot. Let's leave our mothers out of this." She sat up higher in bed, plumped the bolster, fluffed her hair out and put on the "sweet mouth," which was what Moo called the face Camilla Jane made when she wanted something.

"It's hard to leave your mother out of things. She don't miss much," he said.

Camilla Jane looked like she was dividing pecan pie and figuring out how to get the biggest piece without showing it. She said, "I guess you'll just have to cross your heart and hope to die so I can tell you." He crossed his heart.

"Elliot, come here and give me a kiss before I tell you." She pointed to the side of the bed next to her, then she patted the sheet.

He could feel himself getting red. The bottom of his belly felt like it did when he went to Baton Rouge and rode up in the elevator. Camilla Jane had been kissing on him since he was a little kid. She'd catch him in the pantry or the closet. Hot, sloppy kisses right on the mouth, and he always got some of whatever she was eating but he didn't care. It just made those kisses different and special. He would have sold his mother if he could have stayed with Camilla Jane in her hot room and gotten sloppy kisses all day long. He got up on the bed right next to here. She took his hand and put it on her neck above the ruffles and she kissed him.

He squeezed his eyes shut and dreamed about what he always dreamed about when Camilla Jane kissed him. In the dream he was little but he could even let himself think about what else he was. She hugged him real hard for a long time and she seemed to enjoy it, too. He knew there wasn't too much she didn't enjoy.

She said, "Elliot, you are the best kisser I've ever known." Then she finished the French toast, dropping crumbs all over the bed, turned up her coffee cup and drained the coffee in one swallow, some of it running down the dimple in her chin and ending up as a light-brown stain at the top of the white ruffles across her chest. She gave a belch that sounded like it came from her toes, laughed and said, "Better an empty house than a poor tenant," as she stretched her arms up over her head, bowed her back and stretched her feet toward the bottom of the iron bed until her back cracked like a .22.

Elliot moved over to the cane-backed chair next to the bed. "Are you going to tell me or not?"

"Or not."

"Okay," he said, and started out of the room.

"Wait a minute, Elliot," she said very fast, "High John is in the kitchen in the false-bottom drawer of the garde-manger—but don't tell Mama because I need him."

"Why?"

"Mama's sending me to some sort of school in North Carolina to finish me. I can't go there. Took says if I go too far I'll get sick. If I went to New York I'd die."

He laughed at her. "You didn't even have chicken pox when the rest of us did. You're never sick."

"If he wants you sick you're sick; if he wants you dead you're dead. Took said so. I'm scared." And it was on the edge of her eyes.

"Don't believe if you don't want, Elliot, but don't tell where he is. Promise?"

Took yelled up the stairs, "Moo wants you."

Elliot ran out, down the stairs past Took and out the front door. He jumped over the porch railing and headed back down between the two houses. He hid under the hedge to make sure Took was still in the house then went into the kitchen and pulled open the bottom drawer of the kitchen safe. It was a click drawer with a false bottom. He'd watched Took open it a dozen times, whenever there was going to be a party. She kept the good silver oyster forks with the grape leaves in it. He always watched her before he went it. He fancied himself a slick cat burglar, and spying on Took was practice. The latch was on the bottom of the napkin drawer. He pushed the button and the bottom moved back a crack.

It was lying on the second bottom of the drawer looking like this old wrinkled something, like an old dark finger dead a long time. He picked it up and it was just an old root like Moo made medicine tea with sometime—every day and ordinary like Hoodoo, but he felt a warmth in his fingers and an electric feeling up his back like he felt when a magnet moved pins.

He clutched the root and said aloud, "High John the Conqueror, I want to marry Camilla Jane."

He heard Took opening the screen door so he threw High John back in and closed the drawer.

She said, "What you doing here, Creeping Jesus? I thought I told you to go home. What you running your fingers over this time?"

He said, "Moo wants to borrow some damask napkins for Camilla Jane's party."

"Moo got more damask napkins then this house ever seen. You're lying, boy."

All the creases were shook out of Took. She leaned over very slowly and opened the drawer, pressing the bottom latch as she did so. When she saw the High John she shut the drawer and turned to Elliot, looking old in the eyes.

"You poor, dumb little boy," she said. "You already stuck on Camilla

Jane; now you stuck for life. Go on home, Elliot. I can't do nothing for you, and Moo can't either—much as she wants."

Larry Heinemann

Ma'am's Story

It was early October, 1871 in Chicago. A young socialite had been murdered in an upscale bordello on the near Northside. Chicago Police Officer Isham Pepper (a one-armed Civil War veteran) was assigned to the case. After the body was removed and the murder scene sealed for investigation, Pepper visited the kitchen to talk to the downstairs staff. Sarah Pierce, a middle-aged Black woman everyone called Ma'am, ran the household and supervised the cooking. She invited Pepper to sit at the large table in the middle of the kitchen so they could talk. He sat down, stuck the stump of his arm out, and hung the cane there; it was convenient, if peculiar. Then he took out his wallet-sized journal, laid it open, and began asking questions and scribbling notes.

After some time, Pepper abruptly put down his pencil, took a minute to fetch his pipe and tobacco from his pocket, set everything on the table, loaded the pipe with several pinches of shag, and pressed it springy tight with his one good thumb.

"Mr. Pepper," Ma'am said out of the blue, "would you like a cigarette instead." This in itself was odd because Ma'am did not allow smoking-- or snuff, or chew, for that matter--in the kitchen.

"Yes," he said, indeed he would, but rolling was, obviously, not something he could do very well with just the one arm. Ma'am asked Drummond, the yardman, for his makings. Then she proceeded to roll a smoke with a precise care that Pepper had rarely seen. Her daughter Deborah, one of the household maids, and Drummond looked on with a kind of wonder. Finally, Ma'am licked the long edge of the paper, rounded it smooth with her delicate brown fingers, and handed Pepper a cigarette that was as smooth and tight as a tailor made.

"Well, Ma'am," said Pepper. "This has nothing to with any of that unfortunate business upstairs, but I have to know. Where did you learn to do that?"

Pepper spoke for everyone in the room.

And this is the story she told Pepper right then and there:

Ma'am did not know the year she was born, but supposed that she was one side or the other of 40 years old. During her years of slavery, she was owned by a man named Aiden Barrett of Long Oak Plantation on the river near New Orleans. His wife's name was Abigail, and she was mean.

When Ma'am was a child, 6 or 7 maybe, her two older brothers, Crane and Dash, were sold to pay for Mrs. Barrett's and her daughters' trip to the city for the upcoming social season. It was time to present the young women, Patricia and Evangeline, both in the midst of their teens, to society. There would be balls and fetes, promenades and entertainments of all kinds, and many other such opportunities to show them around and get them married off. Ma'am's two brothers, only several years older than she, were sold to a man named Morrison from Texas. A name she would never forgot all her born days. The first time anyone among the cabins had an idea the boys had been sold was the day Mr. Morrison came to the plantation with large wallet of cash and the notarized bill of sale. The brothers wept and struggled so much that Mr. Morrison put them in leg irons brought along for that very purpose, and set them in the wagon. The business was conducted briskly under the great broad ovals of Mr. Barrett's sweet pecan trees. The papers were exchanged. The two men shook hands with wishes of a swift journey home. The boys were sternly admonished to behave themselves and not make trouble (or a whipping it would be). And that was that. Mr. Morrison mounted the wagon, squared his hat, took up the reins, bid Mr. Barrett a good morning, keyed the horses, and drove away. The boys, sitting with their bare feet dangling over the back, were scared and confused and cried more and more, but made no trouble.

"A whipping was, after all, Mr. Pepper, a whipping," Ma'am said.

She watched her brothers as the wagon moved away as steady as you please, their faces ashen and shiny with tears. Finally, the wagon came to the end of the lane, turned onto the road, and passed behind the oleander hedge. All she could remember was Mr. Morrison's floppy straw hat above the thick hedge of bushes. Her brothers, two of Aiden Barrett's own sons not yet 10 years of age, were never seen or heard of again.

"The Lord only knows where they've got to since, Mr. Pepper," she said.

The master, in his shirt sleeves, his fingers spotted with ink, turned and walked through the shade back to the house and his waiting noontime dinner. He never spoke of Crane and Dash again, as if the minute that wagon turned the lane and the dust settled, his memory of them was summarily erased.

Ma'am sat at the table and repeated her brothers' names, Crane and Dash, looking away from her work for a moment and fooling with her account book.

Right then and there, she decided that she had better make herself useful in a very big way. So, she set herself to learn how to roll cigarettes, a new thing back then. The master enjoyed his cigars, but had taken to cigarettes with enthusiasm. It took her a while, but she learned how to roll cigarettes tolerably well. So, Ma'am worked in the kitchen alongside her mother, fetching and carrying, and was at Mr. Barrett's beck and call to make his smokes--among other things.

Meanwhile, Deborah stood with her back to the conversation next to the stove, cutting an apple, arranging it on a plate, set it on the table between her mother and Officer Pepper, and stood near the stove, watching and listening to a story all too familiar to her.

Pepper listened to the story, and admired the cigarette, rolling it between his thumbs and finger. Ma'am struck a stove match with her thumb nail, and lit it. Since he couldn't smoke and write at the same time, there was a long pause while he smoked. They talked of small things, city things. Pepper entertained everyone by blowing smoke rings straight across the table, and everyone watched them curl, rising toward the door.

Then Ma'am got to ask her question, the question, in fact, that everyone in the house wanted to know--Deborah included.

"Mr. Pepper," she said. "Now, let me ask you a question. How did you come to lose that arm?"

"Well, Ma'am," he said, swinging the stump forward so that the cane knocked against the chair. "It was in the war, of course."

Of course.

He had joined the Army of the Potomac, he told everyone in the kitchen, in 1863. In the spring of '64, President U.S. Grant, a general back then and new to those parts, moved the army across the Rapidan River for the last time and pushed south against the Army of Northern Virginia. Pepper had even seen the general once, a little bitty squat looking guy with a big old hat standing next to a beautiful black horse. A rebel cannon took Pepper's arm clean off at a place called Cold Harbor. That, he said, and a piece of his hip, which, of course, explained the cane. Just lucky he wasn't killed, he guessed.

"And what happened to you in the war," Pepper asked.

"Like always, Mr. Pepper," Ma'am said. "Us black folks just worked. The day I remember was the day I went free. The day we all went free, Mr. Pepper. Praise the Lord."

The war had been going along for some years. Aiden Barrett had died years before, and his eldest son, John, was now master of Live Oak. He and his brothers and their older sons were off fighting. Letters home were not plentiful. The youngest brother, Willis, has already been killed, and the grief of his death had settled hard into the big house. There would be more grief, and in plenty, but none of the slaves would be there to see it. There was already plenty of talk of how the southern cause was lost.

Then one wash day Ma'am was out back of the big house scrubbing bed linen. It was hot, sloppy work, like always, so late in the morning when it was time to go inside and get dinner for the big house, she was only too glad. She straightened her back, and turned to the rinse tub to wash the lye soap off her arms when she happened to see a cloud of dust a good way off that rose and hovered above the trees, south yonder. It seemed to move ever so slowly up the road. Well, the first thing that came into her mind was, Lordy, Lord, that must be a dust devil, even though the haze of dust rose high and all but hung in the still, heavy air. She had heard of such things, the Devil come to earth in the form of a swirled up cloud of dust, but she had never seen the like. Then Ma'am turned to the house, and put her attention to making dinner, the big noon meal, along with the rest of the house slaves.

After while, she stepped out on the gallery back of the house, tending to some chore or other, and looked off south again. The dust devil was almost to the saw mill, just there. Then she saw, and hallelujah for that. It was horse men walking along the road nearly to the plantation gate. Union cavalry--flags, ensigns, guidons and all. The air was still, there was hardly a breath of air, and the dust hung above them like a pall. They walked in dust. They passed through dust; dusky men on dusty horses; dusty flags.

Then they turned onto the lane, and lopped toward the house at a right smart gait. Two great, long files of horse men, purposeful and benign. The hooves of many horses, leather and chain bridles, swords, everything rattling with the thick sound of motion, and more dust that drifted with an easy menace toward the house. The ground didn't shake, thought Ma'am just then, but it wanted to. The horse men came a-stomping up to the house, spread out through the yard and garden and on down to the barns and stables, and kept moving until the captain stopped under the grand live oak back of the big house, stood up in his stirrups, reared back, and gave a great shout.

Then he and every one of those horse men swung out of their saddles; more clanking and clattering. When the hubbub calmed down the great cloud of dust they brought with them began settling on every one and every thing, as dry as dry could be. It all but sparkled in the hot, heavy air, and made Ma'am's eyes smart.

From the gallery back of the kitchen Ma'am looked over all the horse men, making a quick count. More than a hundred. Lord have mercy. The yard under the trees was full of horses and men in well-washed blue uniforms, made pale by much use and many miles.

To be sure, it was a fearful astonishment to have the war come into the yard so abruptly. What was more astonishing was that the troopers were all young Black men with dust-covered faces and moist eyes; their dusty shirts soaked through with sweat. She and the other house slaves stood along the gallery with mouths agape.

"What was the world coming to, Mr. Pepper?" said Ma'am.

More than one horse man paused right then and there to drink from his canteen. The horses were also in need of water, and shook lathery spots of dust from their necks, rattling their chain-and-leather tack, stomped their hooves in utter weariness and whipped their long tails for the goddamn flies.

The captain pulled off his gauntlet gloves and slapped them on his trousers. More dust. Then he, another white officer, and two Black sergeants walked over to the gallery back of the kitchen where Ma'am and the slave women stood, staring with trepidacious wonder.

"Good morning, ladies," he said to the women, touching his cap. "Hello, the house," the captain shouted at the door, loud.

After a moment, the elder missus and her daughters came out of the house and stood at the gallery steps just across the way from kitchen garden and the orchard. The women looked fearful. Mrs. Barrett spoke up and asked the officers what was their business with Long Oak Plantation.

The captain introduced himself, John Ash, touching his cap, and introduced Lieutenant Howard Noland. Then he asked the woman's name.

"Abigail Barrett, thank you very much, Captain," she said, "and these were my daughters, Patricia and Evangeline."

The grandchildren of every age went un-named. The women stepped back toward the wicker chairs when the captain and lieutenant mounted the stairs. There was a question about the white men of the plantation, were they in the house or on the grounds.

"All the men were off to the war," Mrs. Barrett said, straight faced.

The captain turned to his men in the yard, and told a Black man named Sergeant Major McCallum to gather all the plantation's slaves to the yard.

He needn't have bothered.

Before the horse men turned up the way toward the house, the field hands, the mill hands, the smokehouse crew and every other slave on the place dropped their work, and made their way toward the house. Something was up. Mr. Lincoln's cavalry was here.

Soon enough almost a great crowd of slaves were mingled in among the horse men, shaking hands, making their way through the crowd, and welcoming them with grateful, open arms.

The captain reached into his dispatch case, pulled out a pamphlet copy of President Lincoln's Proclamation of Emancipation, and read from it to everyone within earshot. Every face turned to listen. The horse men had heard it more than once, but never got tired of it. Ma'am said that when he got to the part about all persons held as slaves... shall be then, thenceforward, and forever free, a great shout went up among the slaves. Whatever else the captain read was lost in a joy that could scarcely be expressed. The reading went on for some time. The captain had a wonderful loud and clear, even booming, plumy voice. The timbre all the more palpable and remarkable under the shade of the pecan and live oak trees. A shudder moved through the crowded yard and gardens like a sudden chill.

"We were free, Mr. Pepper," said Ma'am. "Don't that make you shiver with joy?" Then the shiver became a commotion as men and women broke through the crowd and headed for the cabins down along the creek.

Mrs. Barrett and her daughters understood immediately what was going to happen next, and gathered closely to one another. The children were confounded with fright because of all the horses, the noise, and commotion. The house slaves, women and boys, threw down their rags and chores, and went back into the house to fetch what few things they could lay claim to.

Then the captain said in that clear, loud voice of his that the troop would water their horses, eat some lunch, and return to New Orleans from where they'd come. If anyone wished to accompany them, they were welcome. That's when the pandemonium broke out.

"It was now or never, Mr. Pepper," said Ma'am.

Robert, one of the stable hands, took Sergeant Major McCallum aside. The overseer, Mr. Fleming, a man famous for his whipping arm and sharp attitude, was hiding in the cellar under rug in the front hall. Without so much as a word to the captain, the sergeant major buttonholed half a dozen troopers, and made their way through the crowd to the house. The men walked straight into the kitchen with their pistols drawn, moving along with hard purpose. Their boots made a mean and serious sound that had never been heard in that house before--not in Ma'am's hearing, anyway. They marched straight to the hallway, threw back the rug, and there was the trap door. One of the horse men swung it open, and there was Mr. Fleming, sitting on a cider keg, holding his hat. Two soldiers reached in and grabbed him by the shirt and pulled him straight up out of there. The others fetched along the all the cider, the whiskey and wine, and the several tote sacks of silverware, jewelry, and other such things. Mr. Fleming was hauled roughly through the kitchen, off the gallery, and all but shoved through the crowd of horse men and just liberated slaves, through the kitchen garden and into the orchard. A crowd of ex-slaves and horse men followed along behind. Sergeant Major McCallum shouted for one of the horse men to mount up and come along.

Robert hurried off to the carriage house to fetch Mr. Fleming's braided leather lariat; thirty foot long, or something like.

"This was what we got our whippings with, you understand, Mr. Pepper," said Ma'am. When Mr. Fleming gave out a whipping, man, woman or child, the wrists were tied together with an old piece of leather tack. The slack between the wrists was hooked over a spike nailed in a rafter with a blacksmith's maul. Younger folks simply dangled in the air. Older folks had to stand on their tiptoes. The only man among the slaves who took his whippings standing on his own two feet was Robert, a large, barrel-chested man who had a knack for carpentry and blacksmithing.

Just then Robert came through the crowd into the orchard with the lariat, doubling it down and doubling it down, just like Mr. Fleming would do.

Robert said that a sound whipping was the least that Fleming had coming to him, and that he, Robert, knew just how to lay it on. He would have preferred the bullwhip, but couldn't find it just then.

Sergeant Major McCallum had Mr. Fleming by the scruff of the shirt and shoved him back against the thickest sweet pecan tree in the bunch not 100 paces from the house. The sergeant major told Robert not to bother with the whipping, but rather to make a stout loop. A noose knot was quickly wrapped, slipped over the man's head, and cinched tight around his neck, the knot as tight as a tick just under the ear. Mr. Fleming could barely swallow, and looked around at the crowd with those large eyes of his. Ma'am had never seen eyes so large. Then the sergeant major tossed the bitter end of the rope over one of the high, stout branches, and it swung to the ground. One of the horse men picked it up, and was about to give it to him, but the sergeant major motioned to the mounted horse man, and told him to tie it off on the saddle. This was done. Without wasting another moment, he waved at the horse man, and told him to haul. The horse man backed his horse, and the slack drew tight. The leather squeaked against the bark. The branch bent under the weight, and Mr. Fleming was drawn to his full height in the thick orchard grass. The horse leaned back, keen at the ears. The horse man backed it still, urging the animal with soft jerks of the reins, quite words, and a touch of spurs.

One loud catch of breath came from the gallery.

The lariat went tight, and then the knot went tight as it drew Mr. Fleming to the toes of his boots. With a look of utter desperate panic he was lifted clear of the ground and into the air to the very tips of the grass. He kicked with his legs. He grabbed the lariat with both hands. His face reddened. His shirt stretched against his belly. He kicked his legs more. He made those deep throaty sounds like a man trying to hawk up a piece of something that had gone down the wrong pipe, choking.

"You wouldn't think so delicate looking a thing as a braided leather rope would hold the weight, but it did, Mr. Pepper," said Ma'am. And with plenty to spare.

The horse men and liberated slaves stood around the tree, Ma'am and Deborah among them, watching Mr. Fleming hang, thrashing and red-faced, making that awful sound deep in his throat--chalk-halk-halk--kicking the tree, clawing at the braided leather around his throat while that knot just drew tighter, stretching the very skin of his neck. His face took on the deep color of a bruise. No one, of course, moved a finger to help him.

"A long time it took Mr. Fleming to die, Mr. Pepper," said Ma'am. He thrashed and wiggled around like a bug on a hook. He struggled and struggled, and struggled some more, shuddering, and then his body gave out and hung in the air like a bag of rags, as still as still can be. It was a marvel. It was horrible. The horse men just watched, stone-like and stoic. Many of them were ex-slaves themselves, and thought only that the son of a bitch got exactly what was coming to him. It made everyone else sick to watch it, but no one standing there--fascinated and grateful and appalled--said a thing.

"That man didn't get anything he didn't deserve," Ma'am said, "and make no mistake about that, Mr. Pepper." But it made Ma'am sick to watch it. It made Deborah sick. It made Robert sick. And all that while, the captain and lieutenant made themselves scarce in the house, helping themselves to the cider and what was left of the noontime meal laid out on the table getting cold, and woolgathering through the downstairs rooms. Other folks turned to practical matters, busying themselves with gathering up what little they could carry, hitching the horses and mules to wagons and carriages, clearing out the cabins, and otherwise making ready to leave. Some of the horse men and other folks calmly ransacked the big house pantry, the smokehouse and stock pen. Mrs. Barrett, her daughters, and the grandchildren sat in the wicker chairs and benches arrayed on the gallery, staring intently down the way under the trees at the gate. Their world was vanishing before their eyes. The shock of it took the very air out of their lungs, and turned their faces pale with fret.

"None of us Black folks said much of anything to them," said Ma'am, "and they didn't say all that much to us. After all, Mr. Pepper, what was there to say?"

Well, soon enough the horses were watered and rested, the kitchen garden picked clean, the lunch eaten, the barns and out-buildings emptied of everything easy enough to tote, the big house bedding and linen, drapes and clothes, kitchen ironware and dishes, mirrors and furniture and whatever else would fit in the wagons and tote sacks. It was time to go. The wagons, buggies, and carriages gathered near the house, piled high. By and by the captain gave another great shout. The horse men swung into their saddles all in one motion, and the flags shook out. The captain gave a great round wave of his arm, shouted again, and everyone moved off toward the road and southward New Orleans. Some of the folks rode in the wagons and such, some rode two to a mule, some walked.

"But we were free, Mr. Pepper," said Ma'am. "Free as the breeze."

When Ma'am came out of the big house kitchen for the last time, carrying some cooking pots and fry pans in a bunched-up tablecloth, Mrs. Barrett piped up. "What now, Sarah?" was all the old woman said. Ma'am looked at her, and walked right on down the steps and into the yard without breaking her stride, "Well, Mrs. Barrett, if I was you, I'd start with the dinner dishes and the kitchen floor. Oh, and one more thing. Everybody deserves a good bye, Mrs. Barrett. Good bye."

Ma'am sat with Robert in the wagon loaded with the blacksmith tools and the tack room steamer trunks behind a pair of sturdy mules, trying on a pair of Mrs. Barrett's shoes as the horse men and wagons moved toward the oleander hedge and on to the road. At their backs the Barrett women and children sat on the gallery, stunned (as in a dream), and Mr. Fleming's corpse hung limp in the orchard--dead as stone dead ever was.

"We went to New Orleans and started a new life," Ma'am said. "From scratch, you understand, Mr. Pepper, like you make a special Sunday supper pie."

Diane Kramer

Zebra Man

Zebra Man boarded the bus with thunder steps, each foot encased in a cement block of a boot, silver buckles and clasps cinching the black leather securely to his calves. Despite the bulk of his frame, he nimbly took a side seat adjacent to a middle-aged woman, who sat with body and eyes forward, hands folded at rest into her elbows. As this Othello of a man lowered his body into the steel-molded seat, the woman's eyes just as nimbly moved over and about his appearance. His hair, sculpted into an afro-mohawk, crowned a body that stretched a black t-shirt across a weightlifter's chest and biceps. He adorned himself with a punker's chains and earrings and an assortment of piercings; and though his skin showcased a multitude of inked decorations, the stripes that adorned his forearms, like zebra legs thundering across a savannah, commanded all the attention.

An ice of a chill blew from the ceiling vent, swirling around the silver-streaked hair topping The Woman's head. She tugged a loosely knit sweater closer to her shoulders. Leaning toward Zebra Man, she spoke initially with eyes meeting his, next a smile, finally, "You have some interesting tattoos."

His torso registered surprise, pulling back the way some men do as if touched by a physical hand. By the time he answered, she'd rifled through possible causes for his reaction. Her white skin? Her female gender? Perhaps her age, decades older than his. Or simply that she showed enough appreciation for his tattoos to comment.

"Thank you," he replied.

Zebra Man was not offended at her boldness but rather flattered, his thank you shaded by shyness, or was it wariness? Shifting in her seat and crossing one thickened ankle over another, The Woman offered an explanation to the man she nicknamed Z, "My daughter has a lot of tattoos."

Turning slightly, he smiled and nodded, "Oh, really?"

"Yes, seven."

"Do you like them?" Z asked, his voice slow and soft.

"Well, most of them; some, not so much."

"Do they show?"

"Yes and no, depending on what she's wearing. She covers them for work if needed."

"My Dad can't stand mine," Z offered with a tinge of resignation, yet without the self-consciousness one might expect from one stranger to another, "He just doesn't get it."

The woman guessed Z meant more than the tattoos.

"Yeah, some of us parents are like that," she suggested, hoping he would hear in her voice the sympathy she felt. She had known the sting of her own father's criticism: her politics, her career; sometimes seemingly her entire being. She wanted Z to know she didn't disapprove of her daughter and perhaps by extension that at least this one crazy lady on the bus didn't disapprove of him.

The #10 bus snaked in and out of streets congested with rush hour traffic, through blocks of apartments and offices that stretched into the sky and cast shadows on sidewalks below. Approaching an intersection festooned with arrows and lights, Z's wide paw reached up to pull the stop cord, for both his bus trip and their conversation. He strode from seat to door with musical accompaniment, his boots heaving and stomping, his metal ornaments jingling and jangling.

Z turned and bid The Woman, "Nice talking with you" with surprise in his eyes, and "have a good day" with sincerity in his voice. She returned the wish, then watched him through the dust-engraved window as he disappeared across the street and up the hill toward the university, a direction most-assuredly at odds with his appearance.

As the leaves on the overhanging tree branches changed from green to red to brown, The Woman rode the same route every morning and every evening, glancing up as the bus doors opened with each new rider. She never saw Zebra Man again, the overlap of their lives just a few city blocks. She contemplated if Z wondered still about the passenger who spoke that day as she did about him. She had all the reason to disregard him and he to ignore her; instead she simply turned a stare into a conversation.

Sometimes the bus provides a brief respite from the rules of the world—the hodgepodge of strangers forces few expectations on each other's lives. The roles that riders clothe themselves in before stepping on the bus and after stepping off have little relevance in that moving space. Zebra Man and The Woman hadn't spoken as parent and child or white woman and black man, but merely fellow riders on the same bus.

The Woman welcomed these reflections. Her thoughts ran on undisturbed no matter the goings-on in the front of the bus or the happenings in the back; not when a wiry teenager exited and heaved his bicycle off the bus's front rack and pedaled away; nor when the heavy-set man boarded and squeezed past, searching for an empty seat. She paid no heed when the bus driver turned and called out like a worried parent, "Move farther back; can't be standing on those stairs;" or when the grizzled old woman wearing layers of jackets and canvas shoes with toes cut out shifted a dozen plastic bags from one seat to another.

Typically, The Woman looked up and took note, then quietly resumed folding her thoughts over and over like bread dough she would soon bake into a crusty loaf. She regretted not asking Z about the meaning of his zebra stripes. Too familiar, she had worried. She pondered how he emblazoned his beliefs on his skin and how she kept what was important to her tucked behind her own. Perhaps Z, accustomed by the inability to hide his blackness, faced attitudes about tattoos with the same fatalism he did color prejudice. Never needing to become hardened by racism, she had advantaged herself with silent beliefs, trading in short-term gain to escape a disapproving parent. As the disadvantage of her delusion became clear like freshly washed bus windows, her stomach began to sour. She realized both she and Zebra Man hated the disapproval; but Z had found the courage to parade his beliefs before his father. The Woman never learned how to defend her viewpoint when challenged by anyone. She did a lousy job deflecting a boss's criticism; she couldn't redirect a friend's biting humor; she couldn't even clarify a lover's misperception. She simply had never developed a thick skin.

On this day, in the Friday twilight, all the familiar bus passengers had arrived at their usual stops and disembarked. After a week of one too many people with one too many expectations, The Woman peered through the window while the bus traveled unfamiliar streets far past her usual destination. As the bus approached a section mid-block where neon lights bathed a string of businesses in carnival colors, she felt certain she was at the right place and snapped the stop cord. With her silver hair catching the rainbow lights pulsating through the windshield, The Woman climbed evenly down the bus steps, strode across the sidewalk, and flung open the establishment's doors. Tapping her shoulder, she declared to the decorated man behind the counter, "I'd like a tattoo, please; a tiny zebra, right here."

Kathryn Lane

Do Turtles Ever Cry?

Nightmares plagued me. Crazy, scary images that vanished in a fog as soon as I was fully conscious. A rapid heartbeat, agitated breathing and an overpowering sense of fear—telltale signs of how bad my brain was messed up.

Again tonight, a nightmare awakened me. Friends had suggested it was the 'night crusher' who visited me. That monster reputed to steal into bedrooms terrifying innocent people sleeping in their beds. Only that most people remembered the horrors of that evil spirit assaulting them. I could not recall a single detail.

So disturbing was the aftermath of my nightmares that I researched the topic. Science explains the night crusher phenomena as a dream-like sleep paralysis state occurring between wakefulness and slumber where the victim cannot move or scream. The reason for the complete paralysis is to keep the sleeper from acting out the actions occurring in the dreams. I experienced the symptoms, the unfathomable fear, the trembling and sweating, yet without traces of images or particulars that my waking mind could hang onto or analyze.

My husband, before he left me for a rich, older woman, had little patience for my nightmares.

"Your problem was growing up in Mexico with those scary wife's tales of La Llorona stealing children from their beds and drowning them in the river in the middle of the night, or those stories about Aztec priests cutting hearts out of pubescent girls to appease the gods or even the goddess Coatlicue herself, the mother of gods, the one with the skirt of serpents. Your suffering comes from the culture you grew up in," he often said.

Maybe he had a point. Maybe it was stories I'd heard as a child. As I worked to regain tranquility after the nightmare that had awakened me tonight, I looked across the room. A large mirror hanging over my teak hardwood dresser reflected the dim moonlight filtering through large louvered shutters on the window behind my bed. The mirror's smoky veneer strangely accentuated my feelings of anxiety.

I got up from bed and wrapped myself in a rebozo. I wrapped it around me like a sarong. Even though I now lived in Houston, the hot and humid climate made it easy to cling to childhood habits, like using a rebozo instead of a robe.

I walked to the dresser, a piece of furniture I'd brought with me from the Yucatan peninsula when I relocated here ten years ago and married a football player I'd met in college. The mirror I'd purchased when I moved to this house. I approached the mirror with hesitancy, almost as if the night crusher might lunge out from the smoky mirror. Without peering into it, I edged tentatively closer to the mirror. My eyes scanned several objects sitting on top of the dresser. A carved granite turtle, contrasting with the hardwood, decorated the top. The granite, reflecting moonlight softly bouncing off the mirror's surface, appeared slightly yellow.

I picked the turtle up, surprised by its coldness in the humid heat of summer. Turning it over, I examined the carving and traced its outline with my fingers to feel the crisp, carved incisions of the head, the stubby legs and a short, thin tail protruding from its body. I never looked at myself in the mirror. Instead I touched the stone terrapin to my face, enjoying the clean, unblemished surface of the slightly rounded granite shell.

Memories rushed through my mind like runoff from a thunderstorm. I was ten years old, living in the Yucatan. A tomboy collecting turtles, tadpoles and frogs. The turtles were my favorites. They could hide in their shells. Like I tried to hide from my father. My protective shell was my mother.

I talked to my turtles as if they were playmates. Living ten miles away from the nearest town, I didn't have other children to play with. I felt a connection to these reptiles with flipper-like legs they could use for swimming. A friend of the family worked with me to train them, training all thirteen of them. They were safely enclosed in the perimeters of my back yard. In the evenings, I would stand at the kitchen door and whistle. Usually eight or nine would answer my call with their slow, deliberate walk. They knew if they responded, a treat of ground meat awaited them. During the muggy wet season, if they obeyed my call, they found watermelon rinds, which they snapped off in succulent chunks with their hook-shaped beaks, acting like the jaws of miniature earth-moving backhoes, while pink juice pooled in small sticky spots on the concrete walkway. If I did not hose the sappy liquid away, hordes of sugar ants would dance around the puddles to carry the beneficial droplets to their underground colonies, leaving the stickiness on the sidewalk.

One sultry Sunday afternoon my father drove his Ford pickup truck into the backyard. In the process of parking it under the shade of a large Ceiba tree, he ran over one of my turtles. The shattered shell, like potsherd left behind by an ancient Mayan civilization, was scattered in a loose pile on the grass. The surrounding blades of grass, heavy with the crushed gooey innards, bent low to the sandy soil. Then I saw the turtle head. It had been severed from the body. I started crying.

"Don't be such a sissy," my father said. "You still have a bunch."

"That leaves me twelve," I cried.

"Twelve like the apostles?" he asked. "That's plenty."

"But you ran over my Christ," I cried. "The thirteenth one was the Turtle Christ."

"For god's sake, what stupidity are you talking?" my father asked. His voice sounded rough and impatient.

Instinctively I wanted to run to my mother.

"She's not here. You can't run to her," he said. His intuition picked up my immediate thoughts. His voice sounded full of hatred. "She spends more time with the idiotic priest at that god-damned church than taking care of us."

"She prays there," I said. "She's told me she talks to miraculous saints at the church. Prays that life will get better."

"That's nonsense," he said. He slammed the door to the truck, banging it as if to solder it to the cabin.

"I will never, ever cry again." My voice frothed with venom. Yet as I said it, I wondered if my turtles ever cried. "Never. Ever. Cry. Again."

"Now that's more like it," he said. "I don't like children who cry."

Unable to sleep after the nightmare awakened me, I walked outdoors. In the hot, dry Texas drought, the Koi pond in my yard became the watering hole for skunks, snakes, possums, raccoons and other nocturnal creatures in need of water.

In the faint moonlight, I saw a slow-moving hump amble across the grass toward the pond. I whistled. My call was ignored. The turtle, untrained to expect food in exchange for answering a verbal signal, continued undisturbed on its path. I walked over and picked it up. It was a small one. It retracted into its protective shield. I took my index finger and traced the perimeter of its shell, feeling its natural smoothness interrupted by bumps and blemishes. I touched the back of it to my face, like I'd done earlier tonight with the granite turtle in my bedroom. Like the stone one, I found tonight's visitor surprisingly cool in the Texas heat.

I walked to the edge of the pond and dropped him in, the splash scaring a couple of frogs resting on lily pads. They jumped in the water for protection. A bull frog, hiding in the cattails and dwarf rushes, made a deep croaking sound to warn others of impending danger.

I sat on a chair on the patio to relax. I vowed to forget the nightmare and enjoy the silence of the night. For an hour or so only the screeches, hoots and shrieks of night owls intermittently interrupted my relaxation.

Voices in the distance, barely audible, broke the stillness. The voices became louder. They were angry voices. Anxiety stirred deep inside me.

Anxiety and fear. I wanted to dash inside my house, but thought they might see me. Instead, I crouched down under the iron patio table, waiting for them to pass.

Two silhouettes outside my fence line were fast approaching.

"Don't tell me you're not unfaithful. You think I'm stupid when I answer the phone and someone hangs up?" a man asked. He was big, probably over six feet and over two hundred pounds.

"You're just a jealous nut," a woman's voice replied. "You're insanely jealous...."

"I'm not going to put up with your damned screwing around," he said.

"You're demented. You need to see a shrink," she said.

"I don't need no shrink," he yelled.

The man lunged at her, throwing the woman to the ground. He hurled his huge frame on top of her, striking her face with his fists. They struggled. She kicked him away. Before she could get up, he was on top of her again. He grabbed her neck with both hands. Her legs thrashed about to dislodge him. She kept fighting. Suddenly her body was still.

The man's shoulders loosened and straightened up like a football player leaving a huddle. He looked around. He squatted down again over her, maybe checking the pulse in her neck. He stood up. He took three or four steps to stand next to her feet. He looked around again before positioning his body to pull the woman by her legs. He toiled until he dragged her body off the path. A dry creek bed ran along the other side of the path. He pushed her body into the creek. Like a rabid dog, he turned and ran in the direction from which they had come.

I was shaking uncontrollably, which made the metal table jingle. To stop the noise, I inched away from the table and crawled on the flagstone floor to my kitchen door. I reached up and turned the knob. After crossing the threshold on all fours, I closed the door behind me, my fingers shaking yet grasping the deadbolt to lock it. Still on the floor, without turning any lights on, I took the phone from the counter and sat on the floor to dial 911.

Tears welled in my eyes and spilled over. I tried to stand up but instead went down on my knees again, not intentionally but out of desperation. Soon I found myself crying so deeply I was choking. I had promised myself years ago, a vow I'd made to myself with my father, as witness, that I would not cry. Not a tear had been shed, not a single tear until tonight. Like a watershed in my life, anguish burst forth. And sorrow. And a lot of other emotions, too. I realized I couldn't stop shaking.

A voice on the phone was asking me for the second time if I was ok.

"Yes, I'm ok," I sobbed. "But I just saw a man choke a woman to death." I hoped that she could understand me through my tears and my Spanish accent.

"Where did you see it?" the operator's voice asked. She spoke in a very composed manner, which calmed me.

"Outside my property line."

"Do you know the assailant?" the voice asked.

"I don't think so," I said. I was confused by the images I saw, but I could not remember anyone who looked like that.

"Do you know the victim?" she asked.

"I don't know."

"Where is the assailant now?" she asked.

"He ran back down the path he had come from."

"Where are you?" she asked.

"Inside my house."

"Are you secure in your house?" she asked. Her voice sounded comforting.

"I think so." I wiped my nose with the back of my hand.

The operator confirmed my address.

"Officers have been dispatched. Also an ambulance."

"Ok." I said.

"Can you tell me if the woman is alive?"

"I don't know, but I don't think so," I said. I was sobbing again. I hoped the operator could understand me. "He shoved her body into the creek."

"You'll be safe," the voice on the phone said. "The police are on their way. Do you want to stay on line with me until they arrive?"

"No, I'll be ok," I said.

"Call again if you need help before the police arrive."

I was not crying out of fear, I realized. It felt like something else, something deeper, something personal. I remembered my mother's suffering, the torment she led at my father's side, her troubled life with such a cruel man. My mother's refuge had been her church, and like a turtle shell, the church provided shelter. The scene I'd witnessed outside my fence triggered childhood memories of my parents.

As I brought my tears under control, images flashed through my mind. I suddenly realized my nightmares had turtles in them. Turtles being beheaded. I got off my knees and stood up. The thought of severed turtle heads haunted me. Then I realized my nightmares contained more details. A quick flash of my father strangling my mother ricocheted in my brain cells. How could I have forgotten what he had done that Sunday night so long ago?

It had been an abominable act. My mother's screams. His accusations of her infidelity. The worst part of it was he almost carried it out to its unspeakable horror had I not interrupted him by bursting unexpectedly into their bedroom that night. My mother's neck bore bruises for weeks. She never attended church again.

A loud siren announced the approach of an ambulance. The whining police sirens played chorus to the ambulance. I walked to the living room and looked out. At least five or six patrol cars stopped at various distances from my house.

I watched policemen get out of their vehicles. My mind was still racing away on images from my childhood. That's when I realized the near strangling of my mother had occurred the same day my father ran over the turtle, the thirteenth turtle, severing its head in the process.

Two police officers stepped up to the front stoop. I opened the door.

"Ma'am, did you call about a possible murder?"

"Yes, sir," I said. My Spanish accent evident as I spoke. "On the path in back by the creek. A man strangled a woman. Sounded like she was his wife. He accused her of infidelity. He pushed her body into the dry creek bed."

"Can we get back there from here?"

"Yes, please find your way through the yard." I turned the outside lights on.

From my kitchen window at the rear of the house, I watched the police comb the area behind my property. They had portable strobe lights which lit up the area like a football field. After an hour or so, the same two officers knocked on my kitchen door. I opened it and stepped outside.

"Can you tell us again what you saw?" one of the officers asked.

I repeated the whole incident one more time.

"Well, ma'am, we've searched the area pretty thoroughly. We don't see evidence of what you describe. We're calling the search off."

"Calling it off? You can't do that. A man strangled his wife," I said. My voice was forceful. I could not believe what he'd informed me.

"There's no dead body," the other officer said.

"But I know what I saw...." I said.

"No evidence of a struggle, either," the first policeman said. "If you see anything else, give us a call. I suggest you get some sleep, ma'am."

They both looked at me like I was crazy.

I stood on the patio watching the uniformed men get back into their vehicles. I continued to stand there until the engines of the ambulance and patrol cars were no longer audible. I stepped back inside my kitchen. I could not believe what they had said. No dead body. I looked out the kitchen window, pondering the possibilities of what had happened. If only I'd had my cell phone with me, I could have taken pictures from under the patio table.

Faint light was beginning to appear over the horizon. I returned to the patio, to watch the sunrise. Waiting for the sun to pop up, I thought about my nightmares. They were not a product of my cultural background, as my husband had often voiced. No, they were a product of my childhood. My midnight monster was not the night crusher. My monster was worse than that.

A slight rustling sound sent chills down my back. My first thought was the murderer had returned. For me this time. I couldn't move. My nerves were on the fringe.

The rustle of leaves again. My eyes followed the sound. It was the little turtle who had managed to climb out of the pond and was walking through the papyrus grass, moving the dry blades out of its path.

Barbara Lewis

from Sherrod Village: A Memoir

I am three years old. I am pretty. I have long hair and I only want to wear three plaits and a bang. Mary Joyce likes to put my hair into a whole lot of little plaits like the kids with nappy hair. But I don't want anybody to see me look ugly like that, so I fight with her. I scream until Mama takes the comb and brush and does my hair herself.

Mama thinks I am pretty, too. She never tells me that, but I hear her tell Miss Louise. "She looks just like her daddy," she says. Mama is always bragging about how smart I am. She teaches me to speak proper English. I can count to one hundred in French. We go everywhere together, especially to the Ritz Theater on Reid Street on Friday nights when Daddy is at his poker game.

Today I am all dressed up. I have taken a bath in Sweetheart soap and it isn't even Sunday. I don't know where we're going, but it must be some place special. I have white ribbons in my hair. I wear my navy blue pleated skirt, my white blouse with the rounded collar, my navy blue sweater, my patent leather Sunday shoes and my white lace socks.

Mama holds my hand as we walk. I skip. I am happy. I am lucky, too, because I have my mama all to myself. James Earl has to share his mama with three other kids. He is my best friend.

Mama walks real fast. We cross Carroll Street and walk down. Pretty soon we pass Green St. Then Viola. Then Vance...and Academy. I can see the Center on Reid Street and I tug at Mama's skirt. I want to go play on the swings. "Not today," she says, and we keep walking. When we reach Faison Street we stop. Mama brushes my hair back with her hand. She makes me spit out my bubble gum. St. Alphonsus Catholic Church is on the left. We head towards the building on the right.

When we get there, Mama talks with a lady that smells good. I have seen her before. I saw her walking one day, I don't remember when, but I remember that her long dress flapped in the wind and made her look like a big, black crow.

I don't know why, but Mama leaves me with this lady. She takes me into a room where a lot of other kids are. I do not know any of them. They are bigger and older than I am. I turn to run back to my mother, but she is gone. The big crow lady grabs my shoulder and guides me to a chair. "This is your desk," she says. I start to cry, I do not know what anyone else is doing, but I am crying hard. Nobody asks me what's the matter. I can't believe my mama would leave me here. What did I do? Is this some kind of punishment? Maybe she found out about the eggs I put in my mud pies. I feel lost. I am so hurt. I feel like Mama does not love me anymore, so she gives me away to the black crow. I cry until I go to sleep.

Much later, Mama comes back to get me. She and the crow talk a little while. Mama holds me by the wrist. I can hear her voice as we walk home. I do not understand her words, but I know I am in trouble.

Part One

I was raised in dirt road, out house, stewed chicken feet poverty--poverty so intense that it developed its own personality, its own odor. It had a way, this poverty, of camouflaging itself and making us believe that things were the way they were supposed to be. Most of my classmates and I did not realize how poor we were until we grew up and started to progress (or not). Some of us stayed forever, but a lot of us left--escaped, you might say. Either way, we came to recognize that we had grown up in a bubble that feigned a protection from the real world.

Wilson, North Carolina, was a small, dusty, tobacco town with a railroad track that divided it into *colored* and white neighborhoods. Colored and white schools. Colored and white businesses. Colored and white toilets at the bus station, train station, and courthouse. We knew little about the white side of town except that you had to go there to buy groceries or pay the light bill or shop for clothes and shoes. And regardless of your heritage, if it was non-white, you lived and went to school in the colored section of Wilson.

Of course, our parents had access to the white settlement because many of our mothers worked in service; our fathers were yard boys. For many years my own mother worked at Jimmy Dempsey Laundry, sorting the dirty clothes of people who naturally assumed that black people were supposed to clean up after them and handle their filth. Because they did not know better, some of our parents simply submitted to this new kind of slavery. They had families to feed, and they had not yet entertained the notion that it is better to live freely as a pauper than to wallow in the lap of oppressed luxury. They considered it luxury to work for "good" white folks, to take home leftover ham and cake with which they could feed their own families, and to accept with beaming pride the outgrown shoes and clothes. These they would polish, or starch and iron, and give to their kids for school or church, and if there were items they could not use, they hand-delivered the pieces to someone less fortunate than they in our neighborhood. This was done with an air of benevolence and the absolute expectation that the favor would be returned.

The houses on our street were all the same. Some people called them *shotgun houses*; we called them *inways*. I suppose it was because if you went in one way and walked straight through you'd come out the other way. There was a front room, a middle room, and a kitchen. The spigot was on the back porch, and the outhouse was a few feet away in the back yard. Nearly every family had a grandmother who lived with them, and it was the grandmother who tended the gardens and kept the yard clean. She made yard brooms out of small tree branches, which she tied together with hemp. She took great pride in sweeping the front yard every Saturday morning. The broom made intricate little designs and nobody in our neighborhood—nobody—dared to disturb that pattern without permission. Since there were no telephones, visitors would just stop by, but they would stand at the edge of the yard and holler, "Hoo…wooo." If one wanted company, she'd open the door, wave her arm and say, "Y'all come on in!" If she was busy, tired or sick, she simply did not respond to the holler, and the visitor would continue down the street.

Because there was no living room, the front room was kept ready for company with the chenille bedspread that the lady of the house purchased from the traveling salesman. He kept in the trunk of his car everything a household needed—dishes, glasses, pots and pans—and especially those pink and white rose-designed chenille bedspreads. They cost thirty dollars and he had an installment plan: fifty cents a week or two dollars a month, whichever was more convenient. He and Mr. Vick, the insurance man, were the only ones with gall enough to walk on the newly swept yard, and even they were met at the door with a scowl.

Nothing was wasted in those days. Women often inverted soda bottles into the ground to line the walkway to the house. Boys bent the bottle cap over the tip of a stick and used it as an arrow for fishing or hunting rabbits. Aunt Doretta cut old tires into triangles on one side, painted them white, and used them as yard pots for geraniums. Mama tore brown paper bags into strips and twisted them to make hair curlers. Grandma took worn out socks that could not stand yet another darning and used them as dust rags. She saved buttons and zippers from shirts, pants, dresses and Army uniforms. And each piece that looked like it had no more life in it was cut into squares or rectangles and sewn together to make a quilt. Leftover bread and biscuits were mixed with sugar, eggs, milk and raisins to make bread pudding. The grease from ham and bacon seasoned collard greens and black-eyed peas. Almost everyone had a small garden, and each year they would *put up* tomatoes, beets, peaches and pickled watermelon rinds. I believe my people invented *recycling*.

So this is the way we survived in the days before welfare and food stamps. Not that my parents would have taken such charity—they were both such proud people. My father was illiterate, but he was pretty—

pretty as a girl, almost. He was tall and light-skinned, with wavy hair and a kingly attitude. He was trained in dry wall plastering, and he was good at it. When it rained, and it rained a lot in Wilson, he could not work. So he didn't, because some things were beneath him. Don't get me wrong; he was a hustler. He used to cook at the Do Drop Inn, and the Silver Boot, and the Snooty Fox. He'd come home in the middle of the night and wake us up with a platter of fried chicken and fluffy biscuits, and then we'd all go back to sleep, our bellies full, and our minds content that all was right with the world.

But something broke him. And while I would be a grown woman before I could put it all together, I remember the exact moment it happened.

I am four years old. I have a new little brother. He is different from the last one. The last one was white. I could see through his skin. He did not stay long. One day Dr. Barnes said he was dead. So they took him away. His name was Cornell. This one is dark. They name him Wiley, Jr. I don't think they like him. I hear Grandma Easter say, "He's a fine boy. He just black." Then Daddy gets mad and he beats up my Mama. I scream and beg him to stop. Grandma Easter smiles and walks away.

Today is Friday. Daddy comes home early from his poker game. He hollers at Mama and makes her take me and Jr. to Mrs. Wilson's house. Mama is crying when she leaves us. Me too. I peep out the window. I see Daddy slap her and make her get into the car. They are gone all night. When she comes to get us in the morning, Mama is still crying. Her face is swollen. It looks like she fell down on it. She tells us to be quiet because Daddy is asleep.

Now it is Saturday night. Daddy is leaving for his game. He stands at the front door and hollers at Mama again. He says he will kill her if she leaves the house. All the neighbors hear him say this. When Daddy leaves, Miss Louise comes to our house. She says, "What happened?" Mama put Jr. in his crib. She blows her nose and puts me in the corner to color. "Stay in the lines," she tells me.

I like to color. I mix blue and red to make purple. Orange and green make brown. I sing in French: "Allons enfants de la patria. Le jour de gloire est arrive!" Mama and Miss Louise speak softly, but I hear every word:

"He came home yesterday mad as hell. Somebody told him something. He wanted to take the baby to a doctor for a blood test. I told him, 'Wiley, you can't believe everything you hear in them streets. You know people are always trying to make trouble for other people.' He denied being Jr.'s daddy, just like he denied Barbr'ann. God fixed it so she come here looking just like him. But Jr. is dark. He said, 'Ain't no way a yella man and a yella woman can have a black baby.' He don't stop to think. My daddy was black. His own daddy is black. He just don't stop to think about that."

I stop singing. Mama and Miss Louise look at me. I want to correct Mama's English the way she does me, but I am not supposed to be listening. Besides, I know what she will say: "Don't do as I do; do as I say do." I pretend to be busy choosing a crayon. I hear Mama say,

"So I told him, 'If you gonna take the baby to the doctor, I'm going, too.' I know him, see. He'd come back here, tell me anything and kill me for nothing. So when I said that, he put the baby down, told me to go get in the car. He made me take the younguns over to old lady Wilson's house, and then he took me to the woods, out by the lake. It was dark out there. I was scared. But as God is my witness, my conscience is clear. And I trusted the Lord to save me. He took a piece of rope from the back seat and tied me to a tree. He opened the trunk and took out his shotgun. I watched him load it, praying all the time. But I didn't say a word to him. He sat on the back of the car and pointed that gun at my face all night. He pitched and reared…accused me of all kinds of things. He was a crazy man--crazy! He kept saying, 'Why you do this to me?' Every time I try to defend myself he'd tell me to shut up. I cried. I couldn't help it. I really thought he was going to kill me. I peed on myself. I started praying. I promised God that if He would get me out of this alive, I'd stay and take care of Wiley for the rest of my life. Way after while he untied me, and put the gun away.

"I don't know what I'm going to do. I didn't do nothing." She blows her nose again. She says, "I always loved that nigger much too much, but now…I'm scared of him. I don't want to stay here. But I promised God!" *Then she starts to cry really hard. Miss Louise hugs her. "Lord have mercy,"* *she says.*

After that, everything changed. Every time my little brother cried, or ate, or pooped his diaper, Daddy would holler at Mama. Sometimes he wouldn't go to work. He spent a lot of his time in bed with a legal pad and a pencil, which he used to write down numbers, myriads of them. On Friday nights he would bathe, get dressed in his grey suit and the new shirt that Mama had just bought, tuck two cigars into his jacket pocket, and go off until early Saturday morning. Sometimes he'd come home with a wad of money and make Mama beg for some of it. Other times he'd come home without his watch, or his ring, with nothing but lint in his pockets.

We used to be good friends, Daddy and I. He took me with him on long walks. And then one day, when I was four, he took me to Mrs. Givens' house when Mr. Givens was out of town. He bought me an ice cream sandwich from the truck and left me on the porch swing to eat it while he went inside. When we got home, I told Mama about my day, and Daddy stopped taking me with him after that.

Kathryn Millan

Seeing

Peering at my swing set from inside, I adjust my eyes to the shiny new screen at my nose. Amazing how it disappears when I look past it to our backyard. The light is soft now, it is after dinner. Mother is a good cook and we are sated. She is relaxing in the rocker with the baby, content and happy about her new addition, and proud. We all call him Bicky now, which had become my name for him from a three-year-old's pronunciation. I am glad about that, and proud. Dad is in the other chair enjoying his newly screened porch where we have gathered. He finished the screens this afternoon. His family can now sit out here in the night air, avoiding the Texas summer bugs. He is fulfilled, and proud of this first house for his young family. I realize a new connection as a part of this scene. I finally understand what it is to be a family. It's just us, in a simple moment. We are "Happy and serene," as my mother's later self-proclaimed family motto would wish us to be again.

Stephanie Moore

Two-Faced

I can't save you this time.
I am trying to save myself.
I can't hold you up.
I am the one who needs to be held up.
I can't reach out and give you my hand.
I am trying to hold it together myself.
I can't let you cry out to me.
I am the one crying out.
You are the one who can help me.
You are the one that has a voice.
You have help and refuse to take the hand reaching out.
You turned your back.
You want my help.
I can't save you this time.
I have to save myself.

Ignored

The pain is getting worse.
Do you even hear my cries?
The pain is getting worse.
Does the pain even matter?
The pain is getting worse.
I can not hold onto it much longer.
The pain is getting worse.
It is overwhelming.
The pain is getting worse.
Which way can I turn?
The pain is getting worse.
No one can hear this pain.
The pain is getting worse.
I fall to my knees in exhaustion.
The pain is getting worse.
A hand finally reaches out.
The pain is getting worse.
A shoulder to shoulder some of this.
The pain is receding.
Someone did hear my cries.
The pain is receding.
Someone did see the reason for my lies.
The pain is receding.
The pain did matter.
The pain is receding.
I am no longer overwhelmed.
The pain is not completely gone.
I am no longer alone.

Reaper

The heir to Mombasa has a song that reaches high into the night.
The song is like the music of the streets.
The heir to Mombasa uses the jargon of the people to reach for their
souls.
The heir to Mombasa brings the stragglers home.
The heir to Mombasa is to be watched.
He is a thief in the night.
The heir to Mombasa has a malignant streak.
His malignancy spreads like boils to those who dare stand.
The heir to Mombasa lays the heads on the mattresses of those who ques-
tion his command.
The heir to Mombasa plays the song for the deepest souls.

Fighter

What is it that you want from me?
My heart?
You took that long ago.
My dreams?
You have that as well.
My hopes?
You were my hope.
My son?
No!
He is MINE.
I will fight.
He is myself.
The fulfillment of me.
You count him as leverage.
I count him as my heart.
I count him as my soul.
He is my hopes.
He is my dreams.
He is my everything.
You want to fight?
Be prepared to die.
He is my son.
My love is stronger.
He is worth the fight.
The blood.
The tears.
He is my life.
I will die before I lie down.
You will have to kill me before I let you wrench him from my hands.
I love him more than a body can hold.
You my dear should prepare to surrender.
This mother's love is stronger.

Daniel Peña

Detroit: America's Ciudad Juarez

Even before there was a war in Ciudad Juarez, I remember that Juarez, like much of the border in my childhood 90's, had the feel of a war zone—sublime, heavy, preternaturally charged in its own, unique way. Few other places resonate with the same kind of intensity as Ciudad Juarez. As a child, I swear you could actually feel it, this buzzing tinnitus that framed even the most innocuous of moments: shopping at the Soriana with your mother; watching the Simpson's in black and white with your too many cousins; drinking hot coffee in the morning first thing out of bed, your throat already ignited with morning thirst; the long drives around the periferico; graffiti on the walls outside the car window; young boys and men (and girls) walking to nowhere in particular. It wasn't until I visited Detroit for the first time that I rediscovered this feeling all over again.

Like most young writers/artists/creators who entertain the idea of moving to Detroit, I visited for all of the reasons Patti Smith told me to and also because I'd found a house for one dollar through a Re/Max agent on the internet. I called to ensure the price wasn't a misprint. The agent never called me back but his secretary did. "Yes, the house is really for one dollar," she said, "but of course there will be filing fees. A $1000 deposit and then a $240 inspector fee. You'll need to make repairs, of course," she said. "Some of the houses have solid foundations but mostly they're shells, you know. No back taxes, nothing like that. Altogether, it'll set you back maybe $1500. Would you like to start the process right now?"

If her canned spiel sounded tired, it's because it was. I asked her, frankly, how many calls like mine she'd typically field in a single day. "Too many," she said and left it at that.

The list she sent me was over thirty pages long. I ticked off my potential homes as I drove, choosing the homes I thought sounded best by the street names they were on, street names that my fiancé would maybe like if I told her I'd spontaneously bought us a house in Detroit : Elmhurst, Cherrylawn, Caldwell, Iris Street.

It would be foolish to say that Ciudad Juarez and Detroit are in the same boat—they're not—though it's undeniably true that they're similar. Both are border cities, both rank near the top in most violent cities in the world (Ciudad Juarez at #19 and Detroit at #21) and both, in their own

right, are victims of globalization under NAFTA, a trade agreement rat-
ified in 1994 by Canada, Mexico, and the United States that eliminated
trade tariffs between Canada, Mexico, and the United States in an effort
to spur economic growth through trade.

Under NAFTA, The United States and Canada hoped that the pur-
chasing power parity between their own currencies and Mexico's peso
would allow their respective multinational corporations to manufacture
goods on Mexican soil for cheap, while at the same time being able to
export to goods, tariff free, within the NAFTA trade bloc to bolster prof-
its via the Multiplier Effect. Mexico, in turn, hoped that the agreement
would eliminate tariffs on its own exports while at the same time joining
an already extant trade bloc between the United States and Canada in or-
der to hedge the fluctuating Mexican peso against other world currencies
while, at the same time, bringing jobs to Mexican soil.

So, what could go wrong?

Ask any Mexican farmer whose bushels of corn or gallons of milk
couldn't compete with subsidized U.S. exports; ask any United Auto
Worker Union member in Detroit where his or her jobs has gone and
you'll likely get a better idea.

Back on the road, my F150 lumbers into Dearborn, Michigan, my
tank nearly empty. I liked the idea of coming full circle, of bringing Fat
Elvis (I call her Fat Elvis) back to the place she was made. Dearborn.
My father drove a pickup. My grandfather too. For a lot of Mexicans it's
a status symbol I guess you could say. Manual labor is still strong in my
own family. You're either driving the pickup to the worksite or you're not.

I stop to eat at Tasty Pizza on Ford road. This could be my pizza
joint, I think. This could be my dry cleaners. This could be my grocery
store. What would my grandfather say about all of this? Homeownership.
Suburbia. An F150 right up next to the plant in which it was built. Tasty
Pizza.

I spread out the pages of home listings over the nicked and lac-
quered tabletops of the pizzeria. The teenaged kid who brings me my
slice looks at me with this kind of apprehension, like he wants to say
something but can't. I can only imagine he's seen this scene a thousand
times before—some schmuck with these papers spread out, looking for a
home. "What is it?" I ask, probably too forcefully. In his awkwardness, he
blurts out what we've both secretly been thinking all along. "I wouldn't do
that," he says like some problem-child line from the movies. I hand him
the thirty pages, which he takes between his floury fingers. He ticks off
all the properties that are absolutely out of the question. "This might be
a good one," he says and circles a house selling for five thousand dollars.

"Or this one. Maybe this one. This is by where I live, kind of," he says. "It's probably a safe bet."

I call the Re/Max agent and he tells me that he'll meet me at the property in twenty five minutes but he never comes.

When I get to the house the boy circled, I'm surprised to find that it is barely standing. The paint is nearly chipped off. The home is all jagged slats that look like splintered teeth splayed every which way. Inside the house the walls are gone, the copper piping stripped from inside the plaster. The roof sags. The walls leak. The windows whistle with their untempered glass hanging jagged on the pane, the wind just pushing through without ever lifting so much as a speck of dust.

And in the front yard I wait and wait, that feeling creeping back again, that feeling I'd always thought was so unique to Ciudad Juarez. I hush those feelings in my gut. I try to stymy that tinnitus building momentum between my ears. This is not Juarez, I tell myself. This is not Juarez. But then what if it is? Or if not, then what if it's something similar? An American Juarez? It could happen here too, I think. The sublime of it is already here.

It's just before dark when I decide to leave. My wheels turn past all of the road debris that crunches and pops beneath my tires: blue bottles of dot 3 steering fluid, Styrofoam cups, U.S. Postal Service boxes cartwheeling in the wind.

My gas light flips and I stop for fuel. I'm the only one there besides a group of teenaged boys, three pumps down, filling up milk jugs with gasoline. One of them barks at me. The others bark too. This is not Juarez. This is not Juarez.

I watch as they cross the street to an overgrown park. I watch them pour gasoline over the playground. I watch them as they set the whole damn thing ablaze, just about the same time the stars come out. It's true that even in some cities you can see stars.

Tomás Salas

El Lil' Valentimes

Juliana woke up with intense labor pains on her 21st birthday, Feb. 14, 1977. It was 7am on this bitterly cold Saturday in East Austin, Tejas. She had not slept much in the bedroom with her daughters. She slowly got up without waking her baby girls. Juliana put her robe on over her slip and painfully walked to the other room where Jose was still passed out. He had gotten home after midnight, drunk and angry. Jose had argued with Juliana before she locked herself in the room with their daughters. He was asleep in his boxers under a thin blanket. He had not turned on the space heater. The room was as cold as it was outside. Juliana pulled the blanket off of him.

"Levantate, Jose! You have to take me to the hospital. Ya va nacer el baby," Juliana pleaded. Another contraction shook her petite body and she let out a shrill cry. It startled Jose and he opened his eyes. He scanned the room and figured out the situation.

"Bueno vieja, ya apasiguate. Go get the girls ready," Jose demanded hoarsely from too much drinking and yelling at his wife the night before.

"No puedo. We can drop them off at Olivia's," responded Juliana holding back tears as she staggered out of the room cradling her huge belly.

Jose got up, got dressed, stumbled outside, and started up the car. His reality sank into his foggy brain and he got more anxious than when his daughters were born. The youngest was only 11 months and the eldest two years old. He had trouble believing that it was happening again so soon. He ran back inside to the girls' room, wrapped them in their blankets, and carried one in each arm out to the back seat of the car. He then helped Juliana walk out and get in the front seat.

Twenty-five year old Jose had a wife and two baby girls. Now his third child was about to be born. He was not ready for another baby. Being almost certain it would be a boy this time made him feel a little better.

Jose reversed the '54 Bel-Air out of the yard, threw it in drive and sped out como un loco. He just missed one of their gallinas that had gotten out of the coop. As soon as he pulled out on the street he almost ran over his neighbor's skinny perro.

Jose came to a screeching halt at his sister Olivia and brother-in-law Timoteo's house. He jumped out, grabbed the girls, and ran up the porch steps. He hollered for his sister. She was awake and answered the door immediately. Knowingly, she took the girls without words. Jose ran back and scrambled into the still running car.

Surprisingly, it had snowed for several hours the day before. The thin layer of white dust had not melted.

They slid at every turn. Jose ran three red lights and nearly crashed into two cars that crossed his path while he tried to find the shortest route to Brackenridge Hospital. The blaring horns reminded Jose of his painful hangover. He pressed his foot harder on the gas pedal.

"Chingao, babosos! They need to get out my damn way!" Jose hollered as he swerved around a big red truck.

Juliana knew not to say anything. She did not want to start another fight with her husband. The argument they had the night before had almost turned violent.

Juliana hung on for dear life and silently asked la Virgencita to keep them safe. Gracias a Dios, there was very little traffic that morning. He got them to the hospital in six minutes flat.

Jose Sierra, el segundo, wanted to name his youngest child and first boy, Jose Sierra, el tercero, but his wife Juliana Candelaria Sierra, la primera, knew that it was her turn to pick the baby's name. Jose had already named their first two daughters, Josefina and Joanna, after himself.

All of their names started with the letter J, so if Juliana would not give the new baby his name, then Jose wanted it to, at the very least, start with the same letter. Javier or Joaquin would be a good Chicano name he could live with.

The boy was born on Valentine's Day, the same birthday as his mama's. Juliana wanted to name him Valentine. She thought it would be a sweet name for a boy and besides that, she was very angry at Jose.

Shortly after arriving at the hospital, while waiting for Juliana to be taken to a delivery room, Jose started the argument about the baby's name. He almost yelled at Juliana in front of the other folks in the waiting room.

"Valentine? Estas loca? You must be going crazy, woman!" Joe exclaimed, waving his hands in the air like a crazy vato. He quickly noticed the folks in the room staring at him and without hesitation, he gave them his "what 'cha lookin' at" barrio stare down. Most of them looked away, except for the tiny cinnamon-skinned girl sitting nearby, who thought Jose was the funniest little man she had ever seen. She giggled. Jose could not help but smile when he noticed her, she looked like one of his daughters. He turned back to Juliana, took a deep breath, and lowered his voice.

"Mira vieja, I got a good idea, why don't we name him Valiente, the brave one, yea, algo un poquito mas macho. If we can agree on that, then you can make the final decision," Jose said, thinking he was bien trucha.

"I can make the final decision on the name you already decided on? Mira viejo, you're the one who's crazy. Estas loco or did you eat some weenies con huevos this morning?" Juliana asked sarcastically. The folks who overheard her, smiled. The little girl laughed out loud. Jose did not laugh. He balled up his fists and his ears turned as red as his face. He was so mad he couldn't speak.

Juliana did not look at Jose. She stared straight ahead and to end the argument said, "I am going to give our baby the name I pick for him when the doctor puts him in my arms."

In between the contractions Juliana did her best to remain calm. Why she didn't give in to her husband this time, she was not sure, maybe it was to keep him from trying to control everything, or maybe because he had not mentioned or said happy birthday to her.

Besides the fact that her husband was acting loco and her contractions were so intense, Juliana felt something might go wrong with her delivery. She had a feeling that it would be a difficult birth. Thankfully the nurses came to take her to the delivery room right after she had the last word about the baby's name.

Jose stayed in the waiting area, where a few folks glanced at him out of the corners of their eyes. He was still stewing in his anger and hangover.

It was half past noon and the baby had not arrived. They had been there since 7:30am. Jose's nervios were shot to hell and his head still felt like it was being stabbed with an ice pick. He tried to get excited about greeting his new son, but he was too impatient to wait another agonizing minute.

Without telling anyone, Jose found the closest exit. He bolted out the door and made his way to La Perla, a nearby cantina on E. 6th street. He went to play pool, cure his hangover, and relax his nerves.

Eight ball was his game. Playing billar always put him at ease, especially when he was ganando un poquito de mula, which always happened when he got near a pool table.

Ever since he had returned home from Vietnam, after serving two back to back tours of duty on the front lines, being at a pool table, with a cue stick in one hand and a beer in the other, was the only place he really felt at ease. His heart would finally start to beat, como un reloj, soft and steady. Jose enjoyed being in total control when he was running the table.

Jose, like many of his amigos y primos, had volunteered for the war as soon as he could. He joined the army on his eighteenth birthday. He was placed in the infantry and sent to Vietnam right after boot camp. He turned out to be an excellent soldier. Jose made sergeant in a shorter time than was customary. His superior officers made an exception for him because of his common sense, leadership and bravery under fire. He was awarded the Purple Heart and Bronze Star during his first tour of duty.

Like on the front lines, playing pool was a game where his height, skin color, education, social status, or income did not matter much. It was a game where a chaparito Chicano could show everyone how much of a chingon he was.

It was 2:18pm and he had not returned to the hospital. His first son was born. Yes, Valentine would have been a very sweet and fitting name for her son, but Juliana decided to name the baby, who struggled to breathe on his own, Valentin. She did not name him Valentine, Valiente, Jose, Javier, or Joaquin. She was always reading every book she could get her hands on and had learned in one of them that the name Valentin means strong and healthy. This baby boy had neither and needed all the help he could get.

Juliana was allowed to hold her newborn just long enough to tell him that she loved him, kiss his tiny yellow forehead, and give him the beautiful name Valentin.

Jose won a few dollars playing pool, drank a few cervecitas, and made it back to the hospital at 4pm. He strutted in, feeling bien suave, no longer hung over, and super excited about the birth of his first son. His mood quickly went back to worse than it was in the morning. He was not allowed to hold or see his boy. The doctor had already sent the weak and jaundiced newborn to the hospital's natal intensive care unit.

Juliana's concern had been correct. It had been a traumatic birth and there was some bleeding under the baby's scalp. The doctor had Valentin placed under the blue lights in a glass box that looked like an incubator to hatch pollitos. The lights and pure oxygen would help break down the high levels of bilirubin that turned Valentin's skin and the whites of his eyes a sickly shade of yellow. The doctor assured Juliana that the disorder occured fairly often, was rarely fatal, and that the boy would get well with treatment.

Upon arriving and getting an explanation from a nurse about what happened, Jose immediately blamed the doctor and got madder than a perro con rabia. When the nurse called security, Jose's anger turned into confusion and worry. He could see that Juliana was sad about the baby and mad at him for not being there during the birth. She refused to talk to him. Jose then felt guilt and shame, which gave him the uncontrollable urge to bolt out of the hospital again and go right back to the cantina.

Juliana's three-year marriage to Jose had not been how she imagined it would be. Things seemed to be getting tougher. Their constant arguing had led to stress, depression and anemia during the pregnancy. She now blamed herself and Jose for Valentin's sickness.

The doctor ordered that the baby be kept in the hospital for two weeks and recommended that Juliana stay for a few days to get treated for anemia and nurse her baby. Her daughters would be fine with her sister-in-law. She knew that at this time her boy needed her more than anyone else.

After she was sent home from the hospital, Juliana came to see, hold, and feed Valentin every day for the remainder of the two weeks. On the days when there was no one available to give her a ride, she took two different city buses each way to get to the hospital and back. It was a cold winter and some days the temperature was still dropping below 30 degrees, but this did not keep Juliana from going to care for her son.

Jose worked extra hours at his job and also hustled at the pool tables in the neighborhood bars. The additional money helped cover the extra hospital cost that his insurance was refusing to pay. He hated the insurance companies more than he hated doctors and hospitals. He only went to see Valentin once during those two weeks. The guilt he felt ate away at his heart, but he could not stand to spend any more time in a place where sick and dying people got robbed by those who were supposed to care for them. The second time he went to the hospital was to bring Valentin home, and it was the first time he held the boy in his arms.

Jose was instantly filled with a joy he had never felt before. He finally got to bring his boy home. He was happy, but still not thrilled about the boy's name. Not only was Valentin born small and sickly, now he was stuck with a name that would make him a target for bullies. Jose remembered the Johnny Cash song "A Boy Named Sue." At least, his son could not blame him for the name. He would teach his son how to fight, to be tough and strong.

When they got to their house, everyone that lived nearby was waiting in their yard. They had heard that Valentin was born sick. They were happy he was much better and welcomed him to the barrio. As soon as Jose parked the car he jumped out and opened the passenger door for Juliana and the baby. The happy couple smiled at each other for the first time in long time.

Timoteo, their brother-in-law, moved closer to take a look at Valentin.

"Congratulations, Joe! Glad your boy is doing better. We finally get to meet him. Es verdad que he was born on Valentime's Day and you named him Valentimes?" Timoteo shouted out with a hearty laugh. Like all the other vatos in the barrio, he had to pronounce it Valentime's not Valentine's.

"Hijole mira, he is so chiquito, we have to nickname him el lil' Valentimes." Timoteo said, making everyone, even Jose, laugh.

Valentin the baby boy did not understand what was being said about him. It was the first but not the last time someone would call him "el lil' Valentime's."

Reji Thomas

Art

"Alamo Bay 2013" by Reji Thomas

"New Orleans" by Reji Thomas

"Red Man's Dream" by Reji Thomas

Reji Thomas Retrospective: Claudia Voyles with Reji Thomas

Javier VanWisse

A Writer's Progression

One: Dilemna

Poetry is? Problem is… no general idea on which to hang the words. Form a thought or feeling one wants to convey, then build words around that thought in their proper order.

Two: Heir to Mombasa

Mattress, Stragglers, Heir, Mombasa, Jargon, Music, Malignant: An Exercise

The music wafted gently on the breeze, calling the stragglers from afar. Within, the heir to Mombasa lay reclining on a mattress, malignant with the sweat of those who came before. The breath of the Dragon hid the mass of humanity scattered about as the heir forcefully exhaled his future across the room, his bejeweled hand delicately holding the instrument of his doom. The last of the opium glowed faintly in the pipe's bowl. The jargon in the room faded to a bare murmur as the heir's heavy eyelids closed, perhaps for the last time.

Three: What Is a Number? (An Exercise)

A number is anything you want it to be. It could be the amount of doughnuts you are going to eat at the doughnut shop. Or it could be how many creams you want in your coffee when you go to the drive-through at McDonald's. It could be your place in line or the building number you are looking for. My number is 47. 47 happens to be, simply, my age. That's all.

Four: What Do I See? (An Exercise)

I sit in the shade beneath a tree. I look all around and what do I see? I see birds and trees. I see the sky and the clouds high above me. I see the shade from my tree in a ring around me. As I sit in the shade I see a bright spot of light where the shade used to be. Curious, I look up and see a long line of ants climbing down from the tree. They each carry a little green parasol held high overhead.

I take a close look and what do I see? I see that the parasol is really a piece of leaf from the tree. They carry it down and into the ground and slowly the shade disappears around me. What do they do with this green piece of tree? I reach through my mind and know that soon I will find the purpose of this all.

As I ponder, I soon recall they use the leaves to grow mold for the larder. They won't have to hunt or wander far and wide to find food. Makes sense to me.

Five: *The Stranger*

The stranger standing on the crest of the hill is no stranger to the forest and the stream. He is the bane of the squirrel, the turkey, and the deer.

On his feet are knee-high moccasins of silent leather, hugging his calves and sheathing his feet. His pants are made of the deer. His shirt, made of the said deer's brother, lies loosely upon his lithe, sturdy frame, shielding his shoulders from the weight of the sun. Upon his back is a quiver of arrows and a strong bow of bois d'arc wood, made with his own hands. Crowning his head is a shock of jet-black hair. His heavy eyebrows shield his eyes from the sun's bright glare. His craggy face and square-set jaw are like the leather that clothes him.

His keen brown eyes spy a group of deer in the distance and he steps down the rise into the wood, gliding down the hill with the stealth of an owl on the wing.

Six: Escape

I have no memory of my youngest self.

I am in the living room. I am sixteen and I am stuck watching a movie with the family. I am sitting in the back so I can make a getaway. As I am sitting there I know I do not want to be there.

I carefully rise and quietly work my way to the front door. It is but four steps from the living room to the parlor. From the parlor to the front door is only a few more. Already, I feel unburdened with a wall between me and the family. As I carefully and quietly open the front door and make my escape, I feel a rush of relief as the cool night air refreshes me and beckons me away from the claustrophobia of the obligatory family time.

I quietly close the door and fade into the freedom of the night.

Claudia Voyles

Día de los Abuelitos Muertos

Paternal
It was too cold in Kansas for a girl named America. She latched onto the law school bound soda jerk intent on being the Governor of New Mexico and settled in Texas. Did he start to drink on the dirt ranch of his childhood or did that come with a Landman's success? Mover. Shaker. Drinker. But, once a liver goes, it goes. He left a trust fund to cool her resentment, and America took off to see the world.

Maternal
He looked like James Cagney and he'd seen the world. He blew back into Upshur County like a hot-headed wind and wooed her with dance.

She, the baby herself, nine of nine, she didn't think it would happen to her…

Good at figures, she kept the church's books straight. Good at fashion, she copied the big city outfits. Good at ignoring, she overlooked the temper and the womanizing. Good at denial, she sat on the tumors.

He looked like James Cagney and couldn't see the world without her. He blew his savings on diamonds and Cadillacs to woo her back from death.

H-OWL

I don't know why it caught my eye…what shift in the pattern, what intuition grabbed my Sunday morning bleary attention and made me reach for the binoculars… what looked like a stick of driftwood ruffled in the wind…then one-half of the New York Times Sunday edition later, flapping caught my attention, winged and alive.

The prostatectomy had left Lee gut-shot, unable to lift weight or exert, and tethered to the shore. I solicited neighborly reinforcement and canoe. Invoking Mutual of Omaha's Wild Kingdom, I thrilled to the chill adventure.

He was a yearling Great Horned owl, fish-hooked in an abandoned trot line. Worn out from his own struggle, he accepted the indignity of the cat carrier and the bumpy ride to raptor rehab.

But, who rescued "whoo"? Later that day, golden eyes caught now in my cell phone and offered to party guests otherwise fated to postsurgical gruesome details of catheters and casseroles.

Hazel Ward

"Losing Innocence"

I don't know why I remember this incident, but there it is etched in my memory as if these events happened yesterday. I think I wanted to bury the memory because it was so painful to me to lose my first hero. He was my Uncle Oscar, my mother's brother, and I thought of him as larger than life. He was my hero because he was bigger than my other uncles at 6'3", he never cursed or drank, and he did not womanize the way my other uncles did. His voice was never raised in anger towards his children, his wife, his sisters or his brothers. I adored him....This story begins with Big Sis's money. She carried it tied up in a white handkerchief which she tucked under her breasts when she went to work or she tucked it down underneath the clothes in her chifferobe. There was also a dark wooden trunk filled with her snowy white handkerchiefs, her aprons, buttons of every size and shape, and her jewelry: cameos, rhinestone earrings, a few pieces of colored beads and even tarnished silver chains. She'd hide her money there too, both coins and dollars. Sometimes she'd have two or three dollars; sometimes she'd have 30 or 40 dollars, and sometimes with her combined social security and work money she would have more. This memory surrounds one of the times she had the larger amount of money. She lived with one of her sons, my Uncle Oscar, and his wife Auntie Stella. Her room was small and dark; her bed covered with its kaleidoscopic quilt of blues, reds, greens and purple triangles, squares, triangles and stars; her room was painfully neat with three pieces of furniture the focal point of the room: her mahogany chifferobe, the dresser lined with white lace; on top of it she had heavy azure earrings, bits of thread in every imaginable color, and a matching green malachite cameo and bracelet; her heavy brown trunk set at the foot of her bed. It contained every imaginable treasure—her soft white gloves, the blue headdress she wore from time to time, rings fashioned in what appeared to be old gold, hatpins of every shape and size. I loved lifting the lid of that trunk as it became my fantasy of the life I wanted to lead when I grew up!

Where early October in my small town of Seymourville is generally warm and humid, this day was different. It hinted of autumn chill, and the pecan trees on small front lawns were heavy with the green buds bursting to open their covers. The path winding from the back door of my house, through my Uncle J.B.'s yard and on to my Uncle Oscar's house, was bare of traffic. Only a few scraggly dogs were sniffing the ground and yipping softly at each other. There was no barred gate between the three houses; instead, I could stand in my kitchen, look through the screen door and view the places where we had torn apart the thin wire fencing between the three yards…from back door to back door my cousins and I trooped endlessly, day or night, from one house to the other. Dried weeds sprawled everywhere, profuse in their yellowed splendor; in the corner ditch of my house I could see the green narrow dot's flowing leaves, or my uncle's old banana trees that never grew bananas, or the pointed brown and yellow cattails that fringed the corner fence of Uncle Oscar's house. It was afternoon, and I decided to go visit my cousin, Helen Rose, at my Uncle Oscar's and Auntie Stella's house. I walked to their back door, glancing idly at the coffee grounds scattered around the steps and knocked on the door. Nobody answered my knock, but I could hear crying. I followed the crying which eventually led me to one of the three bedrooms, the one that my grandmother occupied. She was sitting on her bed, hands tucked under a white apron. I could see that she had both her chifferobe and trunk open. She was talking to my Uncle Oscar and crying at the same time. She cried, "ya took my money." "No Nanny," Uncle Oscar replied. Big Sis got up from her bed and looked at her son, "I never thought you'd steal from me…All these years and you could have asked!" He looked at her and then hung his head, "Nanny, I'm sorry; we needed the money, and you never really offer any." I walked away perhaps understanding why this October grayness was like no other.

In later years I replay this moment over and over again. I see the open chifferobe with her white usher's uniform, her blue apron right next to it, the red checkered housedress, and a pair of brogans with two other pairs of black and brown Sunday shoes. She had a black crepe dress with a white collar, a blue duster and two other dresses of burgundy and turquoise. Her one hatbox stood ready to be opened. That day it was closed. This was the only wardrobe she had, and I thought to myself, "She owns so little and she asks for less. Why would you steal from her?" I had no answer to that question and neither did he. I remember when he looked up and saw me standing at her bedroom door he tensed and quickly walked out of the room. I sat on her bed and for a while neither one of us said anything. Then she sighed and put her hand atop my head, "Mae," she said, "I want you to forget what you heard today." "But he was wrong," I protested, "he should not have stolen from you." "I live in his house," she said, I have one of the only three bedrooms in the house. Their kids—the three then—have to sleep in the same room. I wash my clothes on his washboard and hang them on his line. I do not pay for the lights to be on or the heat that we need in winter. What would you have me do?"

I had no answer to give. I just know that when I finally left her bedroom my Uncle was standing outside looking off into the distance, and through a line of trees he saw a group of dogs approaching. He turned serious brown eyes at me to see the trickle of tears slowly, slowly escaping. I could not stop them, although inside I furiously tried to contain my pain. He pulled one of my braids as he lowered himself to the ground and took both my hands in his larger ones. He said simply, "Forgive me and someday you will understand why as a man I could not let my children go hungry. Go home now before the dogs get too close to you."

.

Lowell Mick White

Deep Eddy

In the morning it had been raining, and we ended up stuck behind a caravan of senior citizens, all in big recreational vehicles, all from Washington State, all heading south in the rain. I whipped on down the road, sliding in and out between the campers, and every time I passed someone I could feel Amanda tense up beside me on the seat. She was afraid of the big mining trucks that were heading north. Every time I pulled out to pass, she tapped the floor of the pickup with her right foot, searching for a brake pedal. I did my best to ignore her and drive, and so I drove and I drove, and I counted the RVs, 64 of them in all, I think, and I knew they must all be together because of the big red decals that each vehicle had on its rear. I drove on south, the windshield wipers thudded, and Amanda tapped the floor. Neither of us said anything. Once we got past Whitehorse, the rain stopped and traffic seemed to let up, and Amanda was able to relax a little and fall asleep.

How can you truly tell when someone's desperate?

I didn't see anything then.

And if I had, would I have cared?

Amanda woke up sometime later when I pulled off the road, a small cloud of white dust blowing up and around us. When it cleared I could make out an overflowing red litter barrel and a tarnished length of guard rail, and, beyond that, a valley. A range of mountains rose on the other side of the valley, shaded by clouds. A motor home and a mining truck went by, heading west, north, blowing in more dust. Everything seemed drier, though there were still some muddy puddles in the gravel.

Amanda frowned, still half asleep. "Are we there yet?"

"Those are the Cassiars over there, I think," I said. "And that's, I guess, the Rancheria River."

Amanda looked away at the mountains. She asked, "How much farther to Fort St. John?"

We stayed at a motel in Fort St. John on the way up: hot showers, clean sheets, firm mattresses, cable tv, wireless, cell phone reception, air conditioning.

"I don't know." I said. "Maybe 900 miles. We might make it by tomorrow if we push it."

Amanda rested her head against the window of the truck. The weak sunlight cast a shadow across her face.

She said, "Then let's push it."

I waited a moment. I asked, "You're not getting out?"

"No." Amanda sounded serious.

Oh, well. I was tired of her complaining, but I tried not to let it show. To hell with her. I shrugged and opened the truck door. I collected five bottles—three Labatt's and two Cokes—and a wad of paper from under the seat and carried it all over to the trash barrel and jammed it all in. The turnout was at a bend in the road at the top of a bluff. Below, beyond the guard rail and down, the Rancheria twisted through a wide marshy valley and disappeared off to the northwest. Cloud shadows scudded over the valley. The Cassiars were light gray. Between the turnout and the mountains a single cloud was dropping rain, dark gray streaks that settled into the haze. A car with its headlights on went by, blowing dust, heading northwest to Whitehorse. Yukon plates.

I walked back to the truck and leaned in. I said, "I have to pee."

Amanda sighed. She didn't even open her eyes. She said, "That's fine."

The slope of the bluff was steep and somewhat slippery. It was damp but not muddy, and was covered with hard pale gravels that rolled out from under my feet. I rested against a burned-out stump and caught my breath before sliding the rest of the way down the slope. At the bottom there was a fire ring made of gathered wild stones. Ashes, some beer bottles, and a half-burned throwaway diaper were in the ring. Logs had been rolled up close for seats. A path led down to the river.

I stood up close to an alder and urinated. A big truck of some sort headed south on the highway, and dust swirled at the top of the bluff.

In the silence that followed the truck I heard the river. I buttoned my jeans and followed the path, scrambling over a deadfall and splashing across a little creek coming from the north. The creek disappeared into a thicket, but further ahead I caught a glimpse of open water. I climbed over another deadfall, ducked under some alders, and came out on the banks of the river.

The Rancheria came out of the southeast, headed toward the bluff, and turned suddenly to the west. It flowed past my feet and turned on into the south, dropped into a riffle, and disappeared behind some brush. At the base of the bluff, where it turned, there was a logjam and an eddy. The creek seemed to come in there. The water below was shallow and clear with a sandy bottom. Two smallish grayling cruised the base of the pool.

What pretty water, I thought. Look at those wild fish.

Those grayling have never seen a fly.

I thought, I am the first man to see them.

When I got back to the truck, Amanda was counting recreational vehicles. She had my clipboard and was making a mark every time one passed. Well. I got a beer out of the cooler and walked around to the driver's side and got in.

Amanda said, "You must've had to go pretty bad."

"Yeah, I was looking at the river." I twisted the top off the bottle and took a long drink. My jeans were wet from the knee down and there was a scratch on my face, but I didn't care. I said, "I saw this huge grayling. I want to see if I can catch it."

"Those old people from Seattle just passed us," Amanda said. She tilted the clipboard so I could see it—there were a lot of marks. "Most of them—maybe all of them. They blew dust on me."

"We'll pass 'em again," I said. "They drive slow."

"Yeah, and they'll slow us down."

"I'll go catch that fish and let 'em get ahead of us." I tried smiling at Amanda but she just stared at me.

"Look at this," Amanda said. Again she held up the clipboard with all the marks and slashes on it.

Okay, so there were a lot of RVs. I could see that. So she could count.

"I'll just be a minute," I said.

"Come on," Amanda said. "You've caught enough fish already. Okay?"

I looked away and began digging through the pile of maps on the seat between us.

Amanda asked, "Okay?"

"No...." I found our battered copy of the Yukon guidebook and started thumbing through it. I looked up. "No, really, this grayling is enormous—first I saw two little ones, then I saw the big one. He's never seen a fly before. Nobody's seen him before. It's like a whole new world down there."

"Sure," Amanda said. "Right off the road."

"Yeah," I said. I thought of the fire ring and the diaper. There were people here, somewhere, people came here, passed by here, stopped here, but there wasn't anyone here now, except me. So this was my spot. Mine. I said, "Isn't that great?"

Amanda turned away from me and looked out the window. Two more clouds were dumping rain somewhere near the mountains.

I found our place in the guidebook and started to read. "'DC 663.4....' Hey, I was wrong. We're only about 600 miles from Fort St. John. Six-sixty-three from Dawson Creek."

Amanda still didn't look at me. She said "Well, let's get going."

"No, wait...." I said. I began reading again. "'DC 667—"

"Four more miles already?"

"'DC 667...Litter barrel with view of the Rancheria River to south.' That's where we are."

"We have a GPS," Amanda said. "We already know where we are. So let's go, okay?"

"No, wait...'Rancheria River, fair to good fishing for bull trout and grayling.' Well, I guess. The grayling are there, at least." I looked up. "You should see this grayling, it was huge—"

"There's no such thing as a huge grayling," Amanda said.

"It's bigger than any we saw in Alaska. Over 18 inches, easy."

Amanda shifted in her seat, turned to face me. She reached for my beer and took a sip, and made a face. It was warm. We were out of ice.

"Jon," she said, slowly. Choosing her words carefully. "I'm really tired. I'm even tired of looking at—trees. You know? Everything looks the same. We've driven something like eight thousand miles in the last—"

I said, "It's more like about six thousand."

"Okay! So it's six fucking thousand. I don't really care. I just want to get to wherever it is we're going today, and I want that to be just a little closer to home than we are now. I mean, I guess—I don't know." She sighed. Very dramatic. She said, "Fuck."

I looked over at her and tried smiling again. I guess I was a phony, because I didn't care. I just smiled. I just showed my teeth. Phony. I even took her hand and squeezed it.

I said, "This is what I want to do. It'll just be a few minutes. This fish has never seen a fly before."

Amanda pulled her hand away. "You don't even keep the damn things."

"Catch and release," I said. "All the way."

I got out of the truck, shut the door, and leaned in the window.

"You want to get out and watch?"

"No!"

"Sure?"

"Yes, I'm damn well sure."

I took a step back. So she was pissed. So what. I had a right to do what I wanted to do, too. I stepped around to the back of the truck and looked at her through the layers of glass, and I thought of the trip out: prairies, plains, grasses, rivers, badlands, rivers, mountains, rivers, trees, rivers, trees, bridges, trucks, mountains, glaciers, more trees, more rivers, good roads, bad roads, old people in RVs—ten days from Austin to Anchorage, two weeks in Alaska, and now we were still at least a week away from home. She was tired, of course she was tired, and pissed off, too. But being tired and pissed off wasn't going to get us home any time sooner. I had a right to do what I wanted to do, too, and I right now I wanted to go fishing.

I went back around to the window and said, "We'll get there fine."

"You know," Amanda said, "it would've been a lot easier if you'd just left me back in Whitehorse—then I could've caught a flight home and you could dick around in the woods and play Lewis and Clark all you wanted."

"Aw, come on," I said. But I thought, To hell with her. So she was tired and pissed. "It'll be just a few minutes. Then I'll come back and drive like hell. We'll pass the old people. We'll make it fine."

"I don't think so," Amanda said.

I didn't say anything else—there wasn't anything to say, really. I walked around to the back of the truck again. I looked back at her and I saw her take another sip of warm beer, and I saw her twist the rearview mirror around to watch me. After that I ignored her. I dug around in my fishing gear, and I pulled out a rod, a fly box, some gadgets. When I looked up again I saw Amanda pour the rest of the beer out the window.

When I got into place, the river came straight at me, and then turned, the main current curving toward the south and back into the east. I was a little off to the side of the eddy, where a small current circled around and around, out of the main river, burbling up against the bank, along the little sandbar the creek had deposited under the logjam, and back out into the main current of the river. It was pretty water, clear and cold, and it reflected the sky, the trees, me.

The water seemed pretty deep. I tried looking down through the reflec¬tive surface and even with polarized glasses could only see deep greenish shadows. This was probably the place where fish in this section of the river spent their winters, finning around under the ice and snow, holding in the dark, waiting for spring and breakup.

And I saw then the big grayling float up out of the green—I watched it get bigger and bigger, watched it suck down a bug, a grayish-tan caddis fly of some sort. The fish made a little slurping noise and settled back a foot or so in the water. Two other, smaller grayling appeared and hovered off to the left. They all could stay in the eddy as long as they wanted and the river would always swirl food right up to them.

And I thought, This is why I came on this trip in the first place—to see this, the river, the mountains, the everything.

I thought, This is the way life is supposed to be, always.

This place, this water, these fish. Everything new.

Yeah, I stood there watching those fish for a long time.

Then I took a breath.

I stood holding my medium-weight fly rod with a little fly called an Adams, bushy and gray, tied at the end of the leader. I stepped to the side to put more of the bush between me and the fish. There wasn't much room to cast, but I didn't need to cast far. I worked out a little line and slop-rolled a cast into the eddy. The leader straightened out just enough and the fly dropped softly onto the water.

Nice, I thought. Grayling look up. They like to eat insects off the surface. Good. That Adams sort of looked like a caddis. Good, good.

I held my breath.

And then it was very easy. The eddy brought the fly to the big grayling, who spotted it, rose, finned back in the water for a second, looking at it, and then sucked it down.

I set the hook. The shocked grayling jumped, bored out to the main river, quickly jumped twice more, then again, and then tried to go deep. I was using a heavy leader, though, and I pressured the fish, keeping him near the surface of the eddy. One more jump.

It was very easy.

I knelt over the panicked fish and picked it up. It was slick and iridescent, gleaming in the sun¬light, green and bronze, heavy and fat. It gasped in the air, trying to breathe. The big dorsal fin was swept down but I ran my finger along it, pulled it up. A big, big fin. I measured the fish against my rod, and it covered the writing right up to where it said 5 Weight—it was maybe 18 long, maybe 19 inch¬es, easy 16 or 17, 20 inches if I ever felt like lying.

I tried to work fast. I took out my cell phone and took a quick picture of the fish, and then I removed the fly and got the grayling back in the water, holding it by the tail. In a minute or so the fish wriggled and I let go. It shot back into the eddy, into the shadows, and went deep.

I stood looking at the water—and it was then that I realized that back up on the bluff Amanda was leaning on the truck horn.

And I guess I just missed her.

I climbed up the bluff, breathless, and got to the guard rail at the turnout, and she was gone. My truck was gone. There was a Chevy pickup with Yukon plates parked there, and an old, fat guy with a big head of white hair and a gut spilling out between blue suspenders standing next to the truck—and there was the overflowing trash barrel, and some muddy puddles in the gravel with some of my stuff scattered around. But Amanda was gone, and my truck was gone.

I stood there breathing, trying to breathe, my fly rod pointed out behind me toward the river.

"I guess you're the boyfriend," the fat guy said.

Next to one of the puddles I saw a duffle bag that had held a lot of my fishing gear, and the ice chest. Some of my clothes strewn around, too.

"She said you were down there fishing," the fat guy said. "She said you was maybe lost. I was thinking about going to go look for you."

"I wasn't lost," I said.

The fat guy said, "That gal was really mad."

I asked, "Yeah?"

I pulled out my cell phone to call Amanda, get her back here. No reception, of course. Useless. I put it back in my pocket.

"What're you fishing for?" the Canadian asked.

"Grayling…" I said. "Listen—did she say anything?"

"Just that you were fishing and maybe lost. And I could see she was mad."

She was mad. Yeah. Well, fuck that. I climbed over the guard rail and looked at my belongings. A big bag with my reels, and some fly boxes, and a pair of neoprene waders and boots. A pair of jeans and three or four heavy shirts tossed down on the gravel—one shirt with its sleeve trailing in a puddle. I stepped over and opened the ice chest: four LaBatts, no ice. And Amanda was mad. Okay.

I took one of the beers and stepped over and leaned back against the guard rail. Opened the beer. The big Canadian was looking at me. The breeze ruffled his white hair. A pair of RVs headed south, close together, and dust rose up from the road. Behind me the river, the Cassiers.

The Canadian said, "Well, I guess that gal just ran off and left you."

Diane Wilson

Delbert's Tattoo

So if Grandma had known I was hiding in a empty potato bin and not making myself useful, she'd have said, "Lands a'goshin, child! Ain't you got nothing better to do? That's the terriblest thing I've ever seen !" Then, straight out, she'd have asked for Sister Jackson to come and pray the laziness devil out of me cause Sister Jackson could pray you right out of your socks. Grandma could pray, too, but she didn't trust her prayers on family matters, saying if you're asking Jesus for a Rollsroyce but you only got bicycle faith. Guess what you'll get? A bicycle!

Well, it really wasn't a bicycle Grandma got. Grandma got dead Delbert. But that was years and years ago. Before I was born. Before the Fritos. And just to show the Terrible Times they were in, Grandma said when she and her preaching husband (my Grandpa) and a carload of kids first arrived in Texas they searched every back road and mud infested bayou for just the right church to shower the Holy Ghost on them and they found it in an old Pentecostal church beside a chinaberry tree that kids climbed and hung swings on and halfway around the trunk for no good reason was an old shirt tied up and rotten. In spite of all that searching, though, Delbert, their fifteen year old, unsaved son, was lost to Lucifer and his Legions. First, Delbert slipped towards the tattoo parlor and got himself a big red heart tattooed on his chest, then he definitely faltered when two months to the day that he got his first gun and showed it off in the front yard in a short jacket and boots, with the gun dangling from his hand, Delbert shot himself as he was climbing in a boat and got himself a match to a snake-eyed domino on his brand new tattoo.

Grandma knew the situation. She wasn't fooling herself. Delbert had been drug from the boat to the house and the bullet went clear out his back so he'd been dead awhile. Then she quit thinking with her head. That's the first rule: Hard headed saints need to be crucified in their skulls and soaked with the Holy Spirit! So Grandma let Jesus who was sitting right there on the armchair tell her what to do next. 'Forget that gun, Rosa Belle. Read Mark 16, verse 17!'

Grandma asked Jesus to please forgive her for forgetting the words to that scripture in all the gun commotion. Just let her get her Bible out. So Jesus did and she got her Bible out and thumbed over to Mark and read:

These signs shall follow them that believe. In my name shall they cast out devils, they shall speak with new tongues, they shall take up serpents, and if they drink any deadly thing, it shall not hurt them. They shall lay hands on the sick, and they shall recover.

Jesus said Just grab ahold of your faith, Rosa Belle. HOLD ON HOLD ON. No matter what Lucifer says, believe with all your heart that Life will overcome Death this very hour.

Grandma knew everything Jesus said was true. Jesus didn't lie. Regular folks can't do nothing on their own, but they can if they believe Jesus was working behind the scenes. Miracles weren't hard. Everybody knew that. Miracles came straight from Heaven and there was probably a whole warehouse up there with little slots holding the different miracles. Here's a miracle. And there's a miracle! Why, Delbert's miracle was probably laying in one of those slots. It was the belief in miracles that was hard cause that came from us, natural born sinners all the way from Eve who was the Mother of All Sinners. So if somebody doubted a miracle, a split second later they just made God a liar and God didn't like being called a liar. That would rain down hate and strife.

Grandma said she had heard stories all her religious life of how a sister or a brother had been anointed by the Holy Ghost and layed hands on a cold stilled body--- some dead for ten hours!-- and rose it up from the dead. She'd heard shouting testimonies of how a Brother had levitated in prayer, floated up and left his shoes behind. She had seen anointed men and women in their little church in Oklahoma, wash their faces in poisonous snakes and no harm had come to them. Because they believed. She just couldn't let the Devil distract her with his lies.

So Grandma shoved the creeping mass of hysterical girls out of the kitchen where Delbert was laid out on the table and she wedged a chair against the door knob and waited on Jesus to work behind the scenes. Jesus told her to pray for life, even though death was tempting her to doubt it could take place. The cold hands and face. The blue-tinged lips and finger tips. The gaping bloody hole. The presence of death were the devil's lies. God always responded to prayer. And if He didn't, whose fault was that? Not God's. Look for it elsewhere, Rosa Belle.

Grandma said she looked hell in the eye that day. Oh, the misery and suffering she saw as she tried to pull Delbert back from the clutches of hell. It was so hot in that kitchen that there was a vapor-like stream everywhere and the flames would lap up and fork over her feet. Later when she looked at her shoes, the soles had fire marks where the flames had licked the rubber.

Five hours later Delbert was dead and Grandma was very much alive. Grandma's excuse was Delbert was a bit more dead than she expected and she got in too big a hurry. You can't rush the Lord on deliverance cause the Lord don't wait on you. It's you that waits upon the Lord. So Grandma washed Delbert's chest and face and hands and sat in her old rocker in her old place beneath the sawed off teeth of a swordfish hanging on the wall and read her bible until Grandpa came home. Then the family buried Delbert in his Sunday best and Grandma shoved his gun as far back in the rafters of the washroom as she could shove it. She couldn't do nothing about that tattoo. He was just buried with it.

Biographies and Acknowledgments

Biographies

Fine artist and graphic designer, **Rebecca Byrd Bretz Arthur**, has been writing for over four decades, yet only recently has she begun to share her writing with others. She writes with the passion that is characteristic of her visual work.

Pamela Booton, a longtime Austin resident, is active as an arts advocate and financial consultant. She has served as the Director of the Alamo bay Writers' Workshop, the Project Manager for the oral history documentary, *Seadrift Fishermen Legacy Project*, the organizer of the Texas Louisiana Gulf Coast Shindig, and volunteer for Pine Street Station and The East Austin Studio Tour. Pamela promotes the fabulous writing of Lowell Mick White and the glorious art of Reji Thomas. She lives with her husband Javier VanWisse and their two dachshunds.

Linda Caplin is writing her memoir of a life full of adventure and joy from her travels as a Peace Corps volunteer in Ecuador to a career as a counselor at Austin Community College. Now reflecting by the pool with kids, grandkids, and four legged kids, Linda shares a life well lived.

A songwriter, screenwriter and psychologist, **Lee Edwards** lives on the riverside in Austin, Texas, with his creative partner, Claudia Voyles, and a lot of alligator gars.

Grace Fleming writes novels and short stories embracing themes of cultural mixing, clashing, and melding. She draws from personal experience growing up on the U.S.-Mexico border where nations, ethnicities, races and religions thrive. Grace lives in Austin where she serves as Education Research Assistant and Sociology Associate Professor at Austin Community College.

Ken Fontenot was awarded the 2013 Helen C. Smith Memorial Award for Poetry for his third poetry collection, *In a Kingdom of Birds*. He received an MA in German Language and Literature from the University of Texas at Austin and was awarded a fellowship to study in Germany. His translations of contemporary German poetry been widely published. His other books include *For Mr. Raindrinker*, a comic novel set in 1970s

New Orleans, and a poetry collection, *All My Animals and Stars*, which won the Austin Book Award. A New Orleans native, Fontenot lives and works in Austin.

Born into a family of artists and needle workers, **Lori Spence Gallo-way** has spent much of her life expressing herself through the arts. She has found a new passion for expression in the written word. Lori is currently working on a novel where fiction and non-fiction are blended to tell a personal story.

Lee Meitzen Grue is a Louisiana poet and fiction writer who often writes about New Orleans culture and music. Her published books include *Trains and Other Intrusions: Poems*; *French Quarter Poems*; *In the Sweet Balance of the Flesh*; *Goodbye, Silver, Silver Cloud,* a collection of New Orleans stories; and *Downtown*. The recipient of a National Endowment for the Arts fellowship, prizes in poetry and fiction from Deep South Writers, the Associated Writing Programs, and a PEN Syndicated Fiction Prize, Lee has taught at Tulane University, Westminster College and Xavier University. She has conducted numerous seminars and workshops all over the world, from Barcelona to Paris to Hawaii and back to New Orleans. Lee is former Director of the New Orleans Poetry Forum and the First Backyard Poetry Theatre and is the longtime editor of the *New Laurel Review*.

Larry Heinemann won the National Book Award for his novel *Paco's Story*, which was re-published in 2010, titled *Chuyen Cua Paco*, by the Women's Publishing House of Ha Noi, the first American novel about the Vietnam War to be published in Vietnam. His other books include the novels *Close Quarters* and *Cooler by the Lake*, and the memoir *Black Virgin Mountain: A Return to Vietnam*. Larry's short stories and non-fiction have appeared in *Atlantic Monthly, Harper's, Tri-Quarterly*, and numerous other journals. Larry is Writer in Residence at Texas A&M University.

Diane Kramer is a retired community college counselor from Austin, Texas. She is working on a collection of essays about the kindnesses that people do for others called *Humanity Rides the Bus*; her entry "A Rolling Community" won honorable mention in a contest sponsored by Capital Metro in 2011. She also writes about social justice issues and her article "Different Eyes" appeared in the September 2012, issue of the online journal *Social Justice Today*. Her letters to the editor have been published in the *Austin American Statesman, Dallas Morning News, Texas*

Observer, Time, and the *Wall Street Journal.*

The writing of **Kathryn Lane** is inspired by Latin American cultures and her travel to various countries, and she performs and writes fiction and poetry in both English and Spanish. Her short stories have been published in *Swirl Literary Journal, Arriba Baseball!* and *New Borders Voices: an Anthology.* Kathryn's poems have appeared in *Homeless Diamonds, Primitive Archer, Swirl,* and two editions of the *Austin International Poetry Festival Anthology.* Two chapbooks of her poetry, *A Conversation on India* and *Spirit Rocks,* were published in 2012. Kathryn lives in The Woodlands, Texas.

Barbara Lewis is Professor of English and Assistant Dean of Academic Departments at Austin Community College. She received her PhD from University of Southern California. Proud mother of four, grandmother of thirteen, and great-grandmother of fourteen with two more on the way, Dr. Lewis lives in Del Valle, Texas.

Kathryn Millan has returned to her Texas roots after an exciting New York career in photography and photo editing. Her experience with the *New Yorker, Esquire, Talk,* and other national magazines brought her research and production skills to the forefront. She managed a commercial photo studio and traveled the globe with photographer Richie Williamson for clientele such and Bloomingdale's and Bergdorf Goodman. The Robin Rice Gallery has exhibited her work. Kathryn studied art and photography at the University of Texas with Garry Winogrand, receiving two Ford Foundation awards in studio art. Kathryn is credited for research and writing on *Frida Kahlo: Photographs of Myself and Others,* published by Pointed Leaf Press.

Stephanie Moore, a senior majoring in English at Texas State University, is a lover of film and books of all sorts. She says, "I write from wherever my heart is and enjoy doing so. Emotions put into words."

Daniel Peña is a graduate of Texas A&M University and is a Lecturer at Cornell University. His work has appeared in *Callaloo, The Kenyon Review Online, The Rumpus, The Huffington Post,* and other journals. He is currently at work on his first novel.

Tomás Salas, a third generation Tejano and father of three young adults, loves the process of creating. He is just as happy working as a carpenter as he is writing stories based on his experiences growing up in the

Southwest from Texas to California.

The art of **Reji Thomas** spans a vast range of work from paintings on canvas to architectural embellishments to monumental glasswork. Reji's acclaimed art work, in public places and private collections, is cherished by many around the world. Clients include the Texas State Capitol, the Democratic National Convention, Ann Richards, Barbara Jordan, B.B. King, The University of Texas, Trinity University, Black Arts Alliance, Austin Chamber of Commerce, Texas Medical Association, Dell, Austin Community College, Brackenridge Foundation, St. Edward's University, Ronald McDonald House, Steven Spielberg, Four Seasons Hotel, Concordia College, Human Rights Commission, Holy Angels Catholic Church, the City of Austin Mayor's office, the Texas Governor's office. Her work is in the collections of Mexico's President Carlos Salinas and the Queen of England. And Javier and Pamela....

Javier VanWisse lives in Austin with wife Pamela Booton and dachshunds Rudy and Grady. He works at Barton Springs Nursery and spends his free time gardening, building birdhouses, reading, and now writing.

Claudia Voyles spends her days slinging acupuncture needles and herbs. Prior to this she has only published in professional newsletters, journals, and textbooks regarding the use of Chinese medicine to treat addiction and mental health.

Born in the small town of Plaquemine, Louisiana, **Hazel Ward** is the recipient of numerous awards and honors, including the Woodrow Wilson fellowship and the Ford Foundation grant. The literary and academic communities have greatly benefited from her highly respected publications and presentations. She has taught English at colleges and universities throughout the Austin and Houston areas. Dr. Ward currently serves as Dean of Communications at Austin Community College.

Lowell Mick White is the author the novels *Professed* and *That Demon Life* and the story collection *Long Time Ago Good*. He earned his PhD at Texas A&M University and currently teaches at Pittsburg State University. Former NEA Artist-in-Residence at the federal prison for women in Bryan, Texas, Mick is a recipient of the Dobie Paisano Fellowship and is a member of the Texas Institute of Letters.

Author of *An Unreasonable Woman*, **Diane Wilson** is a fourth generation shrimper who began fishing the Texas Coastal bays at the age of eight and captained her own boat by twenty four. Diane believes that in every person's life they will receive one significant piece of information and what they do with that information will direct the course the rest of their life. While mending fishing nets at her brother's fish house, her piece of information came from a newspaper article that listed her home county, Calhoun County, as the most polluted in the nation. Thus, she began her life as an environmental and human rights activist. She has successfully brought major polluters to zero emission and recently fought to close Guantanamo. She has traveled the world from Seadrift to Bhopal to Beirut to Baghdad and back, pursuing her fight for peace, justice, human rights, and the environment. Fortunately for her readers, she discovered that she had what she refers to as a "knack for writing." She is author of *Holy Roller* and *Diary of an Eco-Outlaw*. Her numerous awards include the *Mother Jones* Hell Raiser of the Month, Lois Gibbs Environmental, Giraffe Project, Jenifer Altman, Blue Planet, Bioneers, and the Woody Harrelson Environmental awards. Co-founder of Code Pink and the Texas Jail Project, Diane also leads the fight for social justice. Her acclaimed writing captures the imagination and conscience of us all.

Acknowledgments

Alamo Bay Writers' Workshop
July 19-21, 2013

Alamo Bay Group
Pamela Booton, Director
Lowell Mick White, Editor
Diane Wilson, Freedom Fighter

Instructors
Diane Wilson, Larry Heinemann, Lee Meitzen Grue,
Lowell Mick White

Moderator
Dr. Hazel Ward

Featured Poetry Reader
Ken Fontenot

The Creative Process
Reji Thomas

Event Artists
Reji Thomas, Pat Taylor, Dino Costa, Rebecca Byrd Arthur

Music
Claudia Voyles and Lee Edwards

Assistants
Sienna Ward and Angelo Vitanza

Registration
Joan Gibbs

Dinner
Little Thailand

Venue
Rio Far Niente

Website
Melinda Ledbetter

Book Sales
Bookwoman: Susan Post and Dana Markus-Wolf

Thanks for all the help!

www.ingramcontent.com/pod-product-compliance
Lightning Source LLC
Chambersburg PA
CBHW070624120726
47909CB00004B/1308